Bewitched
in Oz

Bewitched in Oz is published by Stone Arch Books
A Capstone Imprint
1710 Roe Crest Drive
North Mankato, Minnesota 56003
www.capstonepub.com

Library of Congress Cataloging-in-Publication Data

Burns, Laura J., author.
Bewitched in Oz / by Laura J. Burns ; illustrated by Liam Peters.
pages cm. -- (Bewitched in Oz)
Summary: Sorcery is forbidden in the land of Oz, so for two years Zerie, Vashti,
and Tabitha have practiced magic in secret, fearing that otherwise their talents will
be taken away--but when they are finally exposed they discover that there are more
dangerous secrets in Oz than they ever suspected.
ISBN 978-1-4342-9207-0 (library binding) -- ISBN 978-1-62370-129-1 (paper-over-
board) -- ISBN 978-1-4965-0068-7 (ebook) -- ISBN 978-1-62370-241-0 (ebook)
1. Oz (Imaginary place)--Juvenile fiction. 2. Magic--Juvenile fiction. 3. Children's
secrets--Juvenile fiction. 4. Best friends--Juvenile fiction. 5. Consptiracies--Juvenile
fiction. [1. Fantasy. 2. Magic--Fiction. 3. Characters in literature--Fiction.] I. Peters,
Liam, illustrator. II. Title.

PZ7.B937367Be 2014
813.6--dc23

2013050829

Designer: Kay Fraser

Printed in China by Nordica.
0414/CA21400603
032014   008095NORDF14

Bewitched in Oz

by Laura J. Burns

cover illustration by Liam Peters

Stone Arch Books

. Prologue .

"Zerie Greenapple! Why aren't you done sweeping yet?" Mama called.

Zerie laughed. Her mama's voice sounded amused. She knew perfectly well that Zerie was daydreaming again. Every time it was her turn to sweep the porch, Zerie mostly stood there and stared down the red dirt path in front of the house. If she squinted, she could just make out where it met up with the road of yellow brick out at the edge of town.

Zerie liked to dream about what kinds of people she might meet if she ever went down that road. But her mother and her five older siblings liked to have the front porch clean when they ate dinner there on summer evenings.

"Zerie, I'm coming out there in two minutes and you'd better be sweeping," Mama called.

With a quiet sigh, Zerie picked up the broom again.

Her oldest sister, Zelzah, used to tell Zerie that sweeping was the most important job in the Greenapple house. But now that she was fourteen years old, Zerie realized that her sister had tricked her.

Zelzah just didn't want to do the boring housework herself. She preferred to be out picking apples from the family's orchard, because that's where her new boyfriend worked.

"I have a feeling you could do that a little faster if you wanted to," said a voice behind her.

Zerie jumped in surprise. "Grammy, I didn't see you come outside!" she cried.

Her grandmother smiled, contentedly rocking back and forth on the old wooden porch chair. "I can move quickly for an old lady," Grammy said with a wink. "That's why I know you can move quickly too. In fact, I think you could do the whole porch before your mama even gets out here."

Something in Grammy's tone sent a thrill racing

up Zerie's spine. She tightened her grip on the broom handle.

"I do want to finish fast. I hate sweeping," she admitted.

"Then think about the job being done. Picture the whole porch swept clean and sparkling," Grammy said. "Close your eyes and imagine it. Can you see it?"

Zerie nodded.

"Then do it!"

Zerie gripped the broom, picturing the familiar pattern in her head—left corner across the back to the right corner, then sweep everything toward the stairs in the center and off onto the dirt path.

"What are you doing?"

This time Mama's voice didn't sound amused. This time it sounded shocked—in a very bad way.

Zerie opened her eyes and glanced around. Mama stood in the doorway, frowning at her. The porch was swept clean. Zerie frowned too. She'd pictured the job being done . . . but she hadn't done the actual sweeping. Had she?

"I said you could do it quickly, didn't I?" Grammy's eyes shone.

"Mother! How could you encourage her to do

this?" Mama cried, turning to Grammy. "Zerie was moving so fast I could barely even see her."

"She has the talent," Grammy said proudly. "Just like me."

"Mother, it's forbidden," Mama replied. "You know what happens when a citizen of Oz uses magic—and you had Zerie do it right out in the open! What if somebody saw her?"

"Saw me do what?" Zerie asked. "What's forbidden?"

"Sorcery!" Mama dropped her voice to a whisper. "Princess Ozma has outlawed the use of magic. Only she, Glinda, and the Wizard of Oz can do it."

Zerie's eyebrows drew together in confusion. "I thought they were the only people who even knew how to do magic."

"No, child," Grammy told her. "There has always been magic in Oz. Regular folk have the talent, too. We just aren't allowed to use it anymore."

Zerie scanned the porch floor. It was perfectly clean. But all she remembered doing was a single swipe across the wood. "Do you . . . do you mean that I did magic? Just now?"

"You swept the whole porch in the blink of an eye," Grammy said. "Did you feel yourself moving?"

"Not really." Zerie felt her face break into a grin. "Is that my power? I just imagine things and they come true?"

Grammy laughed, and even Mama smiled. "Not even Ozma has power like that!" Grammy said. "Your talent is the same as mine, Zerie. Speed."

"So . . . I moved fast? Or the broom did?" Zerie asked.

"Both, I think. The truth is, you'll have to learn for yourself how to use the talent. I can't teach it to you, for the power of the magic comes from within each person." Suddenly, Grammy was standing next to Mama in the doorway. Zerie blinked. She hadn't seen the old lady move. "Try a few things," Grammy went on. "Learn for yourself. Or find the others and learn together. Friends are always strongest together." Grammy turned and walked into the house.

"Don't listen to her, Zerie," Mama said anxiously. "Princess Ozma says we mustn't do magic, and she's our rightful leader. Promise me you'll listen."

Zerie bit her lip. She couldn't break a promise to her mother. But she needed to know how she'd swept the floor so fast. She felt as if she might burst unless she figured it out.

"I don't even know how I did it," she finally said. "I doubt I could do it again."

"Good." Mama went inside.

"But that wasn't a promise," Zerie whispered.

.1.

"Where are you going?" Zelzah asked as Zerie jumped
down the porch steps.

Zerie stopped just long enough to give Zelzah's
round-faced baby a kiss. "Vashti needs some help with
the bread basket she's making today. We're going into
the woods to find the perfect branches for the handle,"
she said.

Zelzah smiled. "Have fun."

Zerie felt bad for lying to her sister, but this was the
way it had to be. Since the moment she'd discovered
her talent two years ago, Zerie had been forced to do
a lot of fibbing. She couldn't let Zelzah—or Mama or

Grammy or anybody else in the family—know what she and her best friend were really going to do in the woods.

It was bad enough that Zerie and Vashti practiced magic at all. It would be even worse if the people they loved got involved. Zerie knew her mother wanted her to ignore her talent. It wouldn't be fair if Mama got in trouble because of Zerie.

But how could she ignore her magic? It was the most important thing in her life!

Well, except maybe Ned.

"Hi, Zerie," Ned Springer called as she slowly wandered past his round, red-brick house. Sure, the Springer home was in the opposite direction from the woods. But Zerie knew Ned would be out on the porch that wrapped all the way around the house, tinkering with some clockwork machine. That's where he always was.

Zerie pushed a lock of her curly red hair behind her ear and waved at him. "What are you making?" she asked.

"A cuckoo clock," he replied. "With a hummingbird that comes out and flies around the clock once for every hour."

"Wow. I can't wait to see it when you're done," Zerie told him.

She loved all of Ned's clockwork machines . . . almost as much as she loved watching his strong, bare arms as he worked. Or his thick dark hair, with that one curl that always fell over his soulful brown eyes.

"Where are you going?" came another voice. Ned's younger brother, Brink, peered at her through an open upstairs window.

"Oh, um . . ." Zerie tried to think of a good reason she'd be passing the Springer house on the way to the woods. "I was . . . well, I was . . ."

"There you are!" Vashti Weaver came running up the dusty road. "We should hurry or Tabitha will think we're not coming."

"You're meeting Tabitha?" Ned asked. "Hi, Vashti."

"Hi!" Vashti's smile lit up her whole face, and her dark eyes sparkled.

"Where are you going?" Brink said again.

"Nowhere interesting." Zerie grabbed her best friend's arm. "Bye, Ned!"

"Bye, Ned," Vashti called.

Ned waved as they headed away.

Zerie walked as quickly as she could toward

the forest, which meant sneaking through old Pa Underhill's garden.

Vashti trotted along beside her. "Why were you at the Springers'?" she asked.

Should I tell her that I like Ned? Zerie wondered. After all, Vashti was her best friend. But the very thought of admitting—out loud—the way she felt about Ned made Zerie blush. It was too personal, too embarrassing.

"Why were *you* there?" she asked instead.

Vashti hesitated. "I was looking for you."

Something in her tone made Zerie wonder if that was true. Did Vashti suspect Zerie's secret crush?

"Tabitha really is going to worry," Zerie said, trying to change the subject. "Let's run!"

She took off across Pa Underhill's garden, hopping over the low stone wall along the edge. Vashti laughed and followed, her long black braid flying into the air. Beyond the wall was a small meadow, and then the trees. That was where the two girls stopped, right at the edge of the grass. The forest was made up of thick, red-trunked trees that grew so tall they blocked out the whole sky with their wide, lotus-shaped leaves. Nothing grew underneath them except for nightdrops, a soft carpet of tiny white flowers that covered the floor of the woods as far as the eye could see.

None of the villagers ever went into the forest, because there was nothing to do there—no berries to pick, no animals to hunt, and no paths to follow. The nightdrops spread so quickly that they covered up any path in seconds. It was the perfect place for Zerie and her two best friends.

"Ready?" Zerie asked, holding out her hand.

"Ready," Vashti said. She took Zerie's hand and together they stepped into the forest. "One, two, three, four," Vashti counted the trees they passed.

"Five, six, seven," Zerie went on. "And stop." They stopped and turned to the left. "One step, two steps . . ." Zerie counted their paces until she got to forty, and then they stopped again.

Then Vashti counted twelve more trees as they walked past, and they turned left again. Zerie counted their paces until she reached seventeen. Now they just had to go three trees to the right. It was the only way to find the meeting place that the three friends had agreed on, and Zerie knew all the numbers by heart. Nobody else would ever be able to find them, because nobody else knew the count.

The tiny clearing right next to the third tree was empty.

"I can't believe Tabitha is late," Vashti said. "This must be the first time ever."

A tinkling laugh danced through the air, and suddenly Zerie noticed the nightdrops on the ground crunching as if something heavy was on top of them. Then it happened again.

Zerie gasped. "She's invisible!"

Vashti's dark eyes widened in surprise. "Tabitha? Are you here?"

The laugh came again, followed by Tabitha's face, which appeared slowly, starting from her smiling lips and moving out to show her rosy cheeks, her hazel eyes, and her silky blond hair.

"Can you believe it?" Tabitha asked.

Zerie stared at her friend, who was just a floating head about five feet above the forest floor. "No. And it's a little strange."

"Sorry." The rest of Tabitha appeared, and she laughed again. "I've been practicing every night because my father is away in the Emerald City. And it's paid off!"

Vashti bit her lip, looking worried. "Even if your

dad's not there, you shouldn't do magic in your house. What if somebody saw you through the window?"

"Or didn't see you," Zerie put in. "You know we have to keep our talents secret."

"We've been practicing in secret for two years now, and I've hardly learned anything about using my magic," Tabitha replied. "But in the past week I practiced every day and look at me now." She held up her arm and then made it disappear from the tips of her graceful fingers all the way to her shoulder. "I couldn't do that a week ago."

Zerie felt torn. She and her friends met in the forest every week to explore their magical abilities. Zerie knew she could move fast, but so far all she'd managed to do was run back and forth quickly enough to make a path through the nightdrops. It wasn't a big deal—the flowers grew back over her pathway within a minute afterward. And Vashti's powers hadn't grown much either. When she'd first admitted to Zerie that she had magic, Vashti had been able to make a pebble float about an inch off the ground. These days she could make the pebble float halfway up one of the tall, red tree trunks.

But Tabitha had made herself disappear. That was

a gigantic step forward. Like Zerie and Vashti, Tabitha had first realized she had a talent at fourteen, when she'd made the ends of her fingers fade away until they were almost transparent. In the two years since then, she'd managed to make her feet vanish . . . and that was the last thing Zerie had seen her do, a week ago.

It was amazing how quickly Tabitha's power had grown.

"Did you really learn that just from trying?" Zerie asked. "Nobody showed you how to use your talent?"

Tabitha shrugged. "I haven't been doing anything else," she admitted. "I didn't even brush my hair today." She ran a hand over her golden tresses and winced, even though she looked beautiful, as usual. Tabitha always looked gorgeous.

"Do you think we could do that too?" Vashti asked. "Grow our talents as fast as you did? Maybe we could meet here two times a week instead of one."

"It's hard enough keeping it secret now," Zerie said slowly. "What are you going to do when your father comes back from the Emerald City, Tabitha? You can't keep practicing in the house then."

"I know." Tabitha frowned. "But I can't just stop! I

finally feel as if I'm doing what I'm supposed to do. It's like the old story about Princess Ozma, when she was enchanted and turned into a boy named Tip—remember, the minute Glinda broke the enchantment, Ozma immediately knew who her real self was? That's how I've felt since I made myself invisible for the first time, like I finally know exactly who I am."

Vashti and Zerie glanced at each other and smiled. Tabitha had an old Ozma story for everything. She loved all the legends about the heroes of Oz.

"Don't you feel that way?" Tabitha asked Zerie. "Don't you wish you could be working your magic all the time?"

"More than anything," Zerie said. "I love my talent. I wish we didn't have to hide."

"If we get caught, Ozma will take the talent away, that's what my uncle from the city says," Vashti put in. "He says he saw it once—an enchantress was brought before Ozma and Glinda the Good, and they agreed that she must be punished. The Wizard of Oz took her by the hand and led her into the Forbidden Fountain."

Zerie felt a prickle of fear.

"Into the Water of Oblivion?" Tabitha asked.

"That's the most dangerous substance in the whole Land of Oz. In the old tales, it can even make people forget their own names! They don't really put people in there just for using magic, do they?"

Vashti nodded. "The Wizard put her in the fountain . . . and she vanished beneath the water."

Tabitha's hand flew to her mouth, and Zerie gasped. "But what happened to her?" Zerie asked.

"No one knows for sure." Vashti shrugged helplessly. "My uncle said he saw her again a few days later and she seemed dazed. She didn't remember anything—not the Fountain, and not her talent."

"Can that really happen? My talent feels like it's part of me. Could they really just . . . remove it?" Tabitha asked.

"I don't want to even think about it," Zerie whispered, wrapping her arms around herself. "It would be like cutting off my arm, or my nose."

"How do you think they'd find us, though?" Vashti said after a moment. "I mean, if anyone from the village caught us out here, they wouldn't turn us in, would they?"

"Maybe." Zerie bit her lip. "Maybe Ozma has spies."

"Remember when Bill Pickle got taken away by the Winged Monkeys?" Tabitha dropped her voice to a whisper. "We never did find out how they knew that he was stealing from your orchard, Zerie."

Zerie shivered at the memory of the terrifying monkeys. She knew they were Ozma's servants and that she shouldn't be scared of them. But up close, their eyes had been so black and the sound of their wings so loud . . .

"I don't think it's fair," Vashti said. "Bill Pickle was a thief. He did something wrong. All we're doing is being ourselves and practicing our talents. We don't deserve to be treated the same way."

"That's what my grammy says. Not to me—to my parents," Zerie admitted. "I hear them talking about it sometimes. Grammy has the speed talent, too, and my mama knows about it. But my pop yells whenever Grammy talks about it. He says it's nonsense and that Ozma's rules are always for the best."

"Easy for him to say, he's a man." Tabitha rolled her eyes. "Men don't have magic. What do they know?"

"Well, some men do. The Wizard does," Vashti said. She liked stories about the Wizard of Oz almost as much as Tabitha like stories about Ozma.

Tabitha waved her hand in the air. "Maybe there are one or two around with a talent. But we all know that when it comes to magic, girls rule!" She made her face disappear again, leaving only her wide-set hazel eyes.

Zerie couldn't help laughing. Her friend looked ridiculous. Vashti giggled too. "Stop that! I'm going to have dreams about eyes just floating around on their own."

Tabitha's smile appeared. "Levitate something," she said. "Something bigger than a pebble."

"Okay." Vashti squinted at Zerie's skirt pocket. "Do you have an apple?"

"I always have apples! I live at an orchard." Zerie pulled one out of her pocket and handed it over. It wasn't a huge apple, but it was heavy, and she worried about Vashti trying to lift it. Tiny pebbles didn't weigh much.

Vashti took a deep breath and stared at the shiny red apple in her palm. Slowly, it lifted into the air and began to float an inch above Vashti's hand.

Zerie shot Tabitha an excited look. This was the biggest thing Vashti had ever levitated! "Can you do it without your hand there?" Tabitha asked, her whole body visible now.

Vashti didn't take her eyes off the apple, but she dropped her hand a tiny, tiny bit. The apple wobbled and Zerie had to bite her lip to keep from crying out. But Vashti steadied the apple and then continued to lower her hand, a little at a time, until her hand was at her side and the apple was just floating there all by itself.

"Zerie," Tabitha whispered. "Use your talent. Make it spin."

"What? How?" Zerie asked.

Tabitha reached out and turned the apple gently by its stem. Vashti's eyes grew wide, but she managed to keep it in the air.

"If you make it move faster and faster, it will keep spinning," Tabitha said.

So Zerie concentrated as hard as she could, picturing the shiny red fruit spinning around again and again and again. Faster and faster.

The apple kept moving, twirling in midair.

Zerie felt a grin break out on her face, and she had a feeling that her friends were smiling, too, though she didn't dare move her gaze away from the apple.

Somebody gasped.

The apple fell.

"What was that?" Tabitha cried, turning toward where the gasp had come from. "Did you two see anything?"

The trees had no branches this far down, so nothing was moving. Nothing was out of place. Still, Zerie couldn't shake the feeling that something had been standing between two of the tall red trunks.

"Look!" she cried, pointing to the nightdrops on the ground. They were bent over, but already springing back up. "Someone was here!"

Zerie looked at her two best friends. "Someone was spying on us." Her heart hammered in her chest. "Someone saw us. Someone knows."

.2.

Tabitha ran, following the footsteps before they vanished. Zerie felt frozen to the spot, too terrified to move.

"We're doomed," Vashti moaned. "They're going to drag us off to the Forbidden Fountain and the Water of Oblivion will take away our talents forever."

Zerie felt a burst of anger at that idea. Her magic was a part of her. It wasn't fair that someone could take it away. "I'm going after Tabitha," she said.

She ran as fast as she could, but Zerie couldn't catch up to her friend. In fact, she couldn't even see her.

Zerie slowed to a stop, surrounded by tall red

trees, bright white flowers, and silence. "Tabitha?" she called in a whisper. The nightdrops around her were all standing straight up. Which way had the spy gone? Which way had Tabitha gone?

Zerie closed her eyes. She listened.

Breathing.

Someone was nearby, breathing hard from running. Whoever it was, they were hiding. And the only way to hide in this forest was to stand behind a red tree trunk. Zerie opened her eyes and turned toward the tree three feet away from her. The spy was right behind it, not moving.

Zerie jumped forward, racing around the tree. She knew the spy heard her coming, because there was another gasp and sounds of movement. Zerie got to the other side of the tree trunk to find the nightdrops trampled and a tall figure in a dark cloak hurrying off into the forest. "Come back here!" she yelled.

And then Tabitha appeared right in front of the fleeing figure, materializing out of nowhere.

With a yell of surprise, the boy fell backward and landed on the soft bed of flowers. Tabitha threw herself on his feet to keep him from moving, and Zerie ran over to help.

But the boy wasn't struggling. He looked up at her, his green eyes wide. It was Ned's brother, Brink.

"Brink?" Zerie said. "What are you doing?"

"Hi, Zerie," Brink replied.

Vashti came running up from behind them. Tabitha put her hands on her hips and frowned. "Why were you spying on us?" she demanded.

Brink sat up, his cheeks red and his sandy hair sticking out every which way. "I wasn't spying, I was just . . . watching."

"Well, that sounds even creepier," Zerie pointed out.

"Are you going to tell on us?" Vashti asked breathlessly. "How can we stop him from telling?"

"What? No!" Brink cried. "Why would I tell on you?"

All three girls hesitated. Zerie met Vashti's eyes, then Tabitha's. "Well . . . what did you see when you were watching us?" Zerie asked. Could it be possible that he hadn't seen them using their talents?

Brink sighed. "I saw you standing around and talking?" he suggested. "Just like anyone would in the middle of the forest? Not doing anything at all besides that?"

Tabitha rolled her eyes. "You're a terrible liar. You saw us doing magic," she said firmly. "Why did you follow us?"

Brink glanced around as if he'd like to run away. "I . . . I wanted to see what you were up to," he mumbled.

"Why would we be up to anything?" Zerie demanded. "I told you at your house that we were going to the woods. Maybe we just wanted to take a walk. Maybe we had things to discuss. Maybe we wanted to plan a party. But it's none of your business!"

"I saw you make a sunflower spit out its seeds," Brink burst out. "Two days ago. You stared at it and the seeds all just jumped into your basket."

Tabitha and Vashti glared at Zerie. "You did magic out in your front garden?" Vashti cried. "What has gotten into you two this week?"

"At least I did mine inside the house," Tabitha protested.

"Nobody else was around, it was barely even dawn," Brink put in. "I saw Zerie through the window while I was on my way out to the creek to go fishing. She didn't know I was looking."

Zerie couldn't decide whether to be mad that he'd been watching her or grateful that he was defending her. "You must've been imagining things, Brink," she said. "I pick sunflower seeds every morning. My grammy uses them to make bread. I was just doing my chores the way I always do." It was almost true. She had simply imagined picking the seeds faster than usual, and it had worked. She did a lot of her chores that way when nobody was looking.

"I know magic when I see it," he insisted. "And I thought maybe you girls were coming into the woods to do more. You're always sneaking in here. There has to be a reason."

Vashti bit her lip. "I guess we haven't been as careful as we thought. Does everyone in the village know what we're doing?"

"No," Brink said. "I mean, I don't think so. I'm just especially interested."

Tabitha smiled and raised an eyebrow. "Oh, really?"

Brink blushed. "Yes. Because I have a talent, too."

Nobody said anything for a moment.

"A magical talent," Brink added.

Zerie shook her head. "You're a boy."

"Boys don't have magic," Tabitha agreed.

"The Wizard does," Vashti muttered.

"I didn't believe it either at first, but I do," Brink

insisted. "And I know I'm not supposed to use it, but I want to. I have to. I feel like I'll explode if I don't."

Zerie felt a pang of sympathy for him. She'd always found Brink to be sort of annoying, but what he was saying sounded exactly like something she would say about magic. How would he know how important it was if he didn't really have a talent of his own? "Maybe he's telling the truth," she said, turning to her friends.

Vashti's eyebrows drew together, and Tabitha looked skeptical. "Prove it," she said.

"What?" Brink asked.

"Show us what you can do. You saw us, you know our secrets. So show us yours," Tabitha said. "Or else."

"Or else what?" Vashti whispered.

"I don't know, but I'll figure out something," Tabitha replied. "We can't let him tell on us."

"I already said I wouldn't tell," Brink put in. "I meant it."

"If you really have magic, why are you so afraid to show it to us?" Zerie asked.

"It's just . . . I'm embarrassed," he said. "I've never done it in front of anyone before."

Tabitha crossed her arms and waited. Zerie did, too. Vashti looked scared.

"Fine. I'll try," Brink said. He turned himself slightly away from them, and gazed blankly toward one of the red tree trunks.

"Oh, no!" Vashti cried, "It's Ned!"

Zerie jumped in surprise, and Tabitha spun around so fast that she almost fell over. Ned Springer stood between the trees, the usual dark curl falling over his forehead, the usual smile on his handsome face. Zerie's heart was already beating hard from being discovered by Brink. But seeing his big brother here made her heart pound even faster.

"Ned!" Zerie gasped. "I didn't hear you come up." She automatically ran her hand through her hair to make sure it was fluffed, not that her curls ever really un-fluffed.

"Me either," Vashti said, tucking a strand of dark hair back into her long braid.

Ned gave them a wink, his brown eyes twinkling.

Zerie thought fast. This time they hadn't been doing any magic, so there was nothing to hide. Ned was probably just in the woods to make sure Brink was all right. He was such a good brother! Her own brothers and sisters loved her, but they were far too worried about their own lives to keep tabs on their baby sister. "Did you finish your cuckoo clock?" she asked.

Ned frowned.

"I want to see it when you're done," Vashti cut in, smiling.

"I said the same thing back at Ned's house," Zerie said.

Vashti ignored her. "I love all the clockwork machines you build, Ned."

"Me too!" Zerie said. Why was Vashti acting so flirty with Ned? She'd never even mentioned that she liked clockwork before, and Zerie had known her since they were five. "I've always told Ned how great his clockwork is."

"In fact, I would love to watch you make a whole machine sometime," Vashti went on, shooting an angry look at Zerie. "I think it would be fascinating."

"Well, I don't only like the machines. I like Ned's hair, too," Zerie snapped.

"So do I," Vashti retorted. "And I like his eyes!"

"I like his whole self," Zerie cried. "I like him."

Vashti's mouth dropped open, and Tabitha's eyes widened. Zerie clapped a hand over her mouth, mortified.

What had she just said? Had she really just blurted out her secret in front of everyone? In front of Ned?

Horrified, Zerie turned to look at Ned.

Was he going to laugh at her?

But Ned was gone.

"Where did he go?" Vashti cried, glancing around the forest.

"Oh, no, I scared him off," Zerie moaned. "He ran away from me."

"No, he didn't. He disappeared," Tabitha said grimly. "I was staring right at him and he vanished, the same way I can." She stalked straight toward Brink, and he stumbled back until he was pinned up against a tree trunk, his green eyes wide with alarm. "Does your brother have magical talents too?" Tabitha demanded.

Brink shook his head.

"Then what just happened?" Zerie asked.

Brink's eyes darted toward her for a split second, and then he looked down at his feet. His cheeks were almost purple, he was blushing so furiously. "I . . . I made him appear," he mumbled.

"What?" Vashti said.

"Ned. He didn't disappear. He appeared," Brink

said a little louder. "I mean, I made him appear and then disappear. That's my talent. You wanted me to show you."

The girls all stared at him, baffled. "Your talent is to bring people from one place to another through magic?" Tabitha asked.

"Huh?" Brink looked as confused as Zerie felt.

"How did you get Ned here? And how did you send him back?" Tabitha asked.

"Oh! No, I didn't. I mean, he wasn't," Brink replied. "I mean, that wasn't really Ned. It was an illusion."

"It was not," Zerie said. "It was Ned. He was standing right there. I couldn't see through him or anything. It looked just like him!"

"That's my talent," Brink said again. "I promise."

"Wow." Tabitha stepped away from Brink and he relaxed a little.

"He looked so real," Vashti said quietly. She shot Zerie an embarrassed look. "I can't believe it wasn't really Ned."

Zerie felt a sudden stab of anger and embarrassment. "Why did you do that?" she asked Brink. "If you can make things appear, why did you pick Ned? Did you want me to make a fool of myself?"

"What? No! You didn't make a fool of yourself," Brink said.

"Yes, she did. We both did," Vashti replied. "That was really mean, Brink."

"You said I had to prove I had talent, and I did," he argued. "I only know how to do it with things I see all the time, and I see my stupid brother all the time. It's not like I could make a Hammer-Head appear! I've never met one. But I know exactly how Ned looks, so I can make an illusion of Ned. How was I supposed to know that you two would act all gooey about him?"

Vashti's eyes filled with tears, and Zerie felt her own face grow hot. They had both acted like fools, and all over a pretend Ned! And now everybody knew how she felt about him, and they probably all thought she was ridiculous.

"I'm going home," she said, turning her back on Brink. It was all his fault. Without him and his talent, none of this would've happened.

"Zerie, wait!" Brink called as Zerie walked off through the trees. "Zerie . . ."

But Zerie started to run. No one could ever catch her when she ran.

.3.

"Zerie? Is that you?" Grammy called as soon as Zerie stepped inside. "Wipe your feet!"

Zerie smiled despite herself. Her grandmother had said that same thing every single time she'd come through the door in her entire life. Grammy always seemed to know which Greenapple kid it was just by the sound of their footsteps. And they all had to wipe their feet.

"Okay," she called back, wiping her feet before she stepped into the front parlor.

It felt good to come home, where everything was normal. Familiar. The smell of Grammy's cooking in the kitchen, the music of her brother Zepho's banjo wafting in from the backyard, the faint noise of the apple cart's wheels out in the orchard.

It had been such a strange day. Her talent— and Vashti's, and Tabitha's—had suddenly grown so strong. And her crush on Ned Springer had come tumbling out into the open. And Brink Springer had magic . . .

Zerie closed her eyes and took a deep breath. She would just pretend none of it had ever happened. She didn't want all this change. She wanted things to be normal.

"Hi, Zerie."

Her eyes snapped open. Ned Springer stood two feet away from her.

He's an illusion, Zerie thought immediately. Annoying Brink must have followed her home just to make fun of her for liking his brother. She wasn't going to fall for it.

"Are you okay?" Ned asked, narrowing his eyes. "Zerie?"

"Um . . ." Zerie glanced out the window. No Brink. "Yes. Sure. I'm okay."

Ned was staring at her and frowning as if she might

bite him. "You look a little mad. And you have a . . . a leaf . . ." He reached out and pulled a small leaf from her red curls. The heat of his hand warmed her cheek, and Zerie's heart sped up. She could feel his touch, and smell the clockwork oil on his shirt, and hear the sound of his breath. This was no illusion. Ned Springer was really here, in her house, with his hand in her hair.

Zerie jerked back, and Ned's brown eyes widened in surprise. "Sorry," he said, handing her the leaf. "Were you in the woods?"

"Yes," she answered slowly. It wasn't like she could hide it—the trees had leaves shaped like lotus flowers, and the forest was the only place in all of Oz that had such trees. "We were looking for the perfect branches for a basket." It was the lie she'd told her sister, so she figured she'd better stick to it.

"We? You mean you and Vashti?" Ned asked. "Anyone else?"

"Why? Are you looking for Brink?" Zerie said.

Ned looked baffled. "Brink was with you?"

"No," Zerie said quickly.

Now Ned's expression was even more confused. "Why did you bring him up, then?"

"I don't know," Zerie replied miserably. She didn't want to keep lying about everything, and she definitely didn't want to lie to Ned. "Why are you even here?" she blurted out.

Ned blushed, and suddenly Zerie realized how rude that had sounded.

"He was dropping off the clockwork maid," Grammy said, coming in from the kitchen. "You remember how she kept cleaning the window only on the right side. Ned fixed her left arm as good as new."

"Oh." Zerie frowned. "I thought you were building a hummingbird clock today."

"I was, but I took a break to drop off your maid," Ned said. "I thought maybe I'd catch you and your friends on the way back—you ran off so fast earlier."

Grammy raised an eyebrow. "Maybe you two would like to sit down and have a glass of apple juice," she suggested, steering Zerie into an armchair. "Ned, I'm sure you can spare a few minutes."

"Of course. Thanks." He sat down across from Zerie and stared at his feet.

Grammy thinks he's here because he likes me, Zerie thought.

But she didn't get that feeling from Ned. His eyes kept darting around the room like he was nervous, and whenever she happened to meet his gaze, he instantly looked back down at the floor. Plus, he kept bouncing his legs up and down, up and down, so fast that Zerie could hardly understand how he was doing it.

"Are you sure you want a drink? You seem like you're in a hurry," she said.

"No. Yes, I mean, I'd love a drink." Ned smiled, finally looking right at her. Zerie found herself grinning back. She couldn't help it, he was so cute!

"Thanks for fixing our clockwork maid," she said.

"Not a problem." Ned pulled his chair a little closer to hers. "Zerie, you and I have always liked each other, right?"

Zerie's heart jumped into her throat. Was he telling her he felt the same way she did?

"Right," she whispered.

"So be honest with me," Ned began.

"Here's your juice!" Grammy sang out, bustling in with two big cups of fresh apple juice and a plate of fresh-baked bread. Ned moved his chair back, and Zerie felt a stab of disappointment. Grammy put the drinks down on the little table and handed the bread to Zerie. She gave Zerie a wink on the way back to the kitchen.

"I love your grandma's bread!" Ned grabbed a piece and stuffed it in his mouth. Zerie sighed. Whatever moment they'd been having was clearly over.

"So you were saying . . ." she prodded him.

He nodded. "Right. We're friends, so I know you'll tell me the truth," Ned said.

"Of course," Zerie replied. Not that she'd been doing much truth-telling today, except when she accidentally told all her friends how she felt about Ned.

"Were you and Vashti in the woods with Tabitha?" Ned asked.

Zerie frowned. In an instant, all her thoughts vanished about lying and her friends and Brink's illusion of Ned. "Excuse me?" she asked.

"Was Tabitha there with you?" he repeated.

Why would he want to know that? Zerie wondered, a chill creeping up her spine. Maybe the Springer boys were really spying after all. Maybe Brink had been there watching Zerie and her friends do magic, and maybe Ned knew about it. Had he seen Tabitha using her talent at home? She'd said she was careful, but who knew what Ned could've seen through the window. Tabitha's talent was incredibly strong. She would be the one Ozma would be most interested in. Why else would Ned ask about her?

"I know you three girls spend a lot of time together," Ned went on. "I see you going off toward the forest a lot."

"You're spying on us?" Zerie cried.

"Spying?" he said. "What do you mean?"

"Why are you watching us?" she demanded. "What are you trying to see?"

"Well . . ." Ned hesitated. "Nothing. I'm just trying to figure out what you girls like to do. I know you're all best friends, and so I thought you could tell me what . . . what Tabitha likes to do."

Zerie stared at him for a moment, speechless.

"Never mind." Ned stood up quickly. "I'm sure you have to go help your grandma. Goodbye, Zerie."

He rushed out the front door before Zerie could respond.

"Well, I certainly misread that situation," Grammy said, laughing, from the kitchen doorway. "I thought Ned might have a crush on you, honey, but I guess he likes Tabitha."

"I guess he does," Zerie murmured.

And now Vashti and Brink—and Tabitha—knew that Zerie liked Ned. And it was pretty obvious that Vashti liked Ned, too. But Ned liked Tabitha.

What a mess, Zerie thought. How was she supposed to be around her friends again after this embarrassing day? Was she supposed to tell Tabitha that Ned had feelings for her? Tabitha was such a loyal friend that she knew she'd stay away from Ned just to avoid hurting Zerie.

"You all right?" Grammy asked.

"It's been a strange day," Zerie replied. "I wish I could wave a wand and make it yesterday, when everyone was normal."

Grammy sighed. "Even the magic of Glinda the good sorceress is not powerful enough to do that, I'm afraid."

"I know. I just don't want everything to change." Zerie frowned. "I like my life the way it is, and now Vashti is mad at me, maybe. And Ned likes Tabitha. And Brink . . ."

Her words trailed off. She wished she could discuss Brink's talent with Grammy, but his secret wasn't hers to tell.

"Don't you worry—your friends will always be

there for you, even if you have a few bumps in the road. Friends need one another, they're always strongest together."

"You always say that." Zerie gave her grandmother a smile.

"That's because it's true! You can't stop things from changing, Zerie, but some change is good." Grammy brushed a stray red curl off Zerie's cheek. "You never know what tomorrow will bring."

.4.

The willow tree was scratching at her window again.

Zerie rolled over and buried her face in the pillow, trying to block out the sound. Every time it got windy at night, the old willow woke her up.

"Zerie."

She pulled the blanket up over her ears.

"Zerie!"

The willow doesn't usually talk, Zerie thought sleepily.

"Zerie, wake up!"

She opened her eyes. Her bedroom was empty. She yawned and snuggled back down. Whatever dream she'd been having was over now.

"Zerie!" This time the voice was louder.

Zerie bolted upright in her bed and peered into the darkness. "Who is that?" she whispered, frightened.

"It's me," said nobody. "Oh! Sorry."

Suddenly Tabitha appeared right next to the bed. Zerie gasped.

"Sshhh!" Tabitha hissed. "You'll wake up your family."

"Well, what are you doing just appearing like that?" Zerie complained. "How did you even get in here?"

"I'm invisible," Tabitha pointed out. "I came through the front door and walked upstairs."

"You're getting pretty cocky about your talent," Zerie grumbled.

"I know." Tabitha giggled. "Listen, you have to come out to the woods."

"Now?" Zerie asked. "It's midnight."

"True. But after you left today, Vashti and Brink and I got to talking—"

"Brink?" Zerie interrupted. "You talked to him after that? He completely humiliated me!"

"He was showing us his talent, like we asked him to," Tabitha said gently. "Anyway, we all decided it would be safer to practice at night. Too many people can see us when we go into the woods."

"Well, nobody ever seemed interested before today," Zerie pointed out. "What makes you so sure we can trust Brink? I still think he was spying."

"He has as much to lose as we do. If he gets caught using magic, they'll take him away to the Forbidden Fountain too." Tabitha stood up and held out her hand. "Come on. We were doing something amazing today before . . ."

"Before Brink," Zerie finished for her.

"Wasn't it exciting, though?" Tabitha asked. "All of us doing magic together?"

Zerie thought about it. It had been pretty amazing, what they had done with the apple. "I'm not sure why we never tried to work together like that before," she said. "Grammy always told me that friends are strongest together. But we weren't ready, I guess."

"And you have to admit, Brink's illusion was incredible," Tabitha said.

"I do not have to admit that," Zerie said, but she let Tabitha pull her up out of bed.

"You thought it was really Ned," Tabitha told her. "And so did Vashti. You two wouldn't have acted so crazy if you realized it was just an illusion. Which proves that it was a really good illusion."

Zerie groaned. "How am I ever going to face Vashti again? She likes Ned as much as I do. We acted like idiots, and all over a boy who isn't interested in either one of us."

"You don't know that," Tabitha said.

"Yes, I do." Zerie clapped her hand over her mouth. She wasn't supposed to tell Tabitha about Ned's crush on her . . . was she? She wished she could ask Vashti about it.

"What's going on?" Tabitha asked.

"Nothing. Let's go." Zerie grabbed her cloak and headed for the door. Then she stopped. "Wait. I can't make myself invisible. What if one of my brothers sees me? Zane is such a light sleeper!"

Tabitha bit her lip, thinking. "Could you make yourself move really fast? Maybe if you went quickly, it wouldn't sound like footsteps? You'd be gone before anyone noticed."

"I guess I can try," Zerie said doubtfully. She wasn't sure what her family would do if they caught her sneaking out at night—or practicing magic—but she knew she didn't want to find out.

"I'll meet you outside," Tabitha said, melting into invisibility.

Zerie took a deep breath. Tabitha seemed so comfortable with her talent now, as if it hardly took any work at all. But Zerie still felt uncertain.

She closed her eyes and pictured it: the walk from her room, down the hall, avoiding the creaky board at the top of the steps, downstairs to the front parlor, around the overstuffed chairs, to the front door . . . and out to the yard.

She could see the route in her mind, all the familiar objects of her house shrouded in darkness, the clock-work maid powered down for the night in the kitchen, the little glowworm-lamp shining in the front window where Grammy always kept it. She could imagine herself moving through the house, ending up outside, where the stars were shining bright and the red grass was cool and wet with dew.

"You forgot to close the door," Tabitha said.

Zerie opened her eyes. She was standing in the front yard, just as she'd pictured it. "How fast did I go?" she asked.

"You beat me out," Tabitha replied, softly closing the front door. "I barely even saw you, you were moving so quickly."

Zerie grinned. "Let's go practice magic!"

.5.

Brink and Vashti were already in the woods when Zerie and Tabitha arrived. They had planned a different count of trees this time, one that brought them deeper into the woods. Zerie felt a little hurt to think that her two best friends had made these plans without her—and with Brink Springer.

Still, she was here. She might as well work on her talent.

"Hi, Zerie," Brink said.

"Hi." She didn't meet his eyes, or Vashti's. Vashti didn't say anything, and an awkward silence settled over them.

"Let's get started!" Tabitha chirped. "What should we do? We were all working together earlier, but I'm not sure how to bring Brink's talent into that. Any ideas?"

Nobody said a word.

"Well, what if Zerie made something move really fast and I made it invisible?" Tabitha suggested. "Look!" She plucked a nightdrop, which had opened its tiny white petals wide, making a star shape that glowed softly in the darkness. "What can you do with this?"

Zerie looked at the little flower, then back at Tabitha. "Nothing?" she said.

"Please try, Zerie," Tabitha pleaded. "Remember: Friends are strongest together."

"Don't you quote Grammy at me," Zerie grumbled.

"Maybe if I can make the nightdrop spin, you can keep it spinning, like the apple," Tabitha suggested.

"Or you can make it close up again," Brink put in. "Like it does in the daytime."

"How am I supposed to do that?" Zerie scoffed. "My talent is speed, not flowers."

"Right, but if you speed up the flower, it will close," he replied. "Nightdrops open up at night and close in the morning. So if you make the flower's cycle go faster, you can close up the petals."

Zerie stared at him. "You mean I should . . . speed up time?"

Vashti gasped. "Is that even possible?"

Brink looked startled. "I didn't mean it that way. I only meant you should speed up the flower itself."

"But I only know how to speed things up the normal way," Zerie protested. "By making them move faster."

Vashti laughed. "There is no normal way to speed things up," she said.

"I guess that's true." Zerie laughed, too, catching her friend's gaze. But the instant their eyes met, Zerie remembered the way they'd bickered earlier, sniping at each other over Ned. Embarrassed, she looked away.

"Try it, Zerie," Tabitha said.

"But that's just my talent. I thought we were going to use all of our magic together," Zerie protested.

"Let go of the flower, Tabitha," Vashti said.

Tabitha did.

The nightdrop fell toward the ground—then stopped itself and floated back up. Vashti was staring at it, concentrating hard as she levitated the tiny bloom.

"Well, I don't want to make it invisible when you've never done it before," Tabitha said thoughtfully. "And I can't think of a way that illusions would help."

"Me either," Brink agreed. "But I'm happy to just help Zerie for tonight."

"No, you need to practice," Tabitha said. "You try to create an illusion of something besides your brother, and I'll try to make something invisible besides myself."

Their voices faded into the background as Zerie watched the nightdrop. It was beautiful, floating there in midair. Nightdrops were always beautiful, but somehow being up high, gleaming with its white light, made this one more special. It was as if a star had come down from the sky to float between her and Vashti.

Zerie felt a stab of guilt as she looked at her friend's dark, pretty face, lit by the nightdrop. She and Vashti had never fought before. She wasn't sure how to move past it.

"Are you doing it?" Vashti asked.

"Yes." Zerie shoved everything out of her mind

except the nightdrop. Its tiny petals were unfurled as far as they could possibly be, but she'd seen the flowers all curled up many times. She knew that as the hour grew late, the petals would slowly close, starting from the small, pointed tip and rolling inward to the middle. Then, when all the tips were rolled, the petals themselves would draw together, hugging tight to make a little white ball.

She closed her eyes and pictured that ball. It looked like a teeny-tiny pearl on top of a pedestal of green.

"Zerie! You're doing it!" Tabitha cried.

Slowly, Zerie opened her eyes and looked at the nightdrop, floating gently in front of her, curled into a ball.

"I knew you could," Brink said.

The nightdrop vanished.

"I did it," Tabitha whispered. "I made it disappear."

"Halt! In the name of Princess Ozma!" a harsh voice yelled.

And then something came crashing through the canopy of trees—something large and heavy. Another crash, another figure dropping from the sky. Vashti screamed, and Zerie felt Brink grab her arm and pull, hard.

"Run!" Vashti yelled. "Tabitha, run!"

Brink was tugging on Zerie, yanking her through the trees. She only became aware that she was running when she glanced back over her shoulder to see why Vashti was yelling. Tabitha stood still, right where they had left her. She was staring at something in the forest, something Zerie couldn't see. She nodded, as if someone were talking to her.

"Tabitha!" Vashti screamed again, and now Zerie could make out Vashti's shape huddled up against one of the tree trunks about ten feet away from Tabitha.

"Stop," Zerie demanded, digging her heels into the carpet of nightdrops. "We can't leave them."

Crash! Another dark figure came hurtling through the treetops.

"They caught us! It's Ozma," Brink whispered frantically. "Come on, run."

Why wasn't Tabitha moving? Zerie jerked her hand out of Brink's and rushed back to Vashti. "Vash, let's go," she hissed.

"We have to help Tabitha. She's stunned or something," Vashti said.

She stepped away from the tree and suddenly something came flying in between them. Zerie screamed and Vashti fell backward. A six-foot-tall figure, half-man and half-ape, stood over her . . . and spread its huge, leathery wings.

"Winged Monkey," Brink moaned from somewhere in the darkness. "It's the Winged Monkeys!"

Past the gigantic monkey's armor-clad legs, Zerie could see her best friend lying on the ground. Vashti was sobbing. Zerie's cheeks were wet, too, she realized.

They were caught! They were doomed.

ROOOOOOOAAAAARRRRRR!

The sound, deep and otherwordly, came from everywhere at once, echoing through the branches and bouncing from one tree trunk to another. It was loud enough to make Zerie's teeth vibrate, and without thinking, she covered her ears.

The monkey in front of her was just as startled by the strange sound. It shrieked in surprise and flew up into the air.

"Run," Brink cried.

Zerie lunged forward and grabbed Vashti's hand, hauling her to her feet. Together, they raced through the red trees, trying to follow Brink ahead of them. There was screeching behind them, and the beating of strong wings against the air.

"Don't look back," Zerie told her friend. "Don't look back!"

"Cut to the right, that's the way back to Pa Underhill's garden," Vashti panted.

"Brink! Go right!" Zerie called. She didn't wait to see if he'd heard, she just turned and ran, clutching Vashti's hand.

"Let go! Stop! You said I could trust you!" It was Tabitha's voice, but it was far away now.

Zerie let out a sob as she fled.

The monkeys had Tabitha.

"There! The edge of the forest," Vashti said. "We can hide under the collard greens— they're tall."

Zerie jumped over the low stone wall and immediately dropped to her stomach, crawling under the broad leaves of the collard greens until she was hidden from the sky.

"I don't think it will work," she moaned. "They couldn't have seen us through the treetops, but they knew where we were anyway. They'll find us here, too."

"No, someone must've told them we were there," Brink said from nearby. Zerie felt a rush of relief that he'd made it.

"Where's Tabitha?" Vashti asked. "Where do they have her? Why didn't she run?"

"Why didn't she make herself invisible?" Zerie added.

"Look." Brink crawled over next to them. "Through the leaves. Look up."

Zerie did. Her breath caught in her throat. There, against the moon, floated a humongous black shape. "It's a ship. A Winged Monkeys airship."

Two monkeys, their giant black wings beating the air, appeared, silhouetted against the stars. They flew straight for the airship. And between them, held captive, was a girl.

Tabitha.

.6.

For a long time after Tabitha disappeared into the floating ship, Zerie and her friends were silent. Hot tears ran down Zerie's cheeks, and she felt Vashti crying beside her. Brink was a little farther away, lying still on his back.

Zerie stared up at the stars, the moon, and the monstrous black ship. What were they doing to Tabitha up there? She must be terrified.

"The monkeys are gone," Brink whispered, and Zerie startled at the sound of his voice.

"That's true," Vashti said. "I don't hear their wings anymore, or the screeching. That screeching is so horrible." Her voice dissolved into a sob.

"But the ship is still there," Zerie pointed out. "They've just gone inside."

"It means we can move, though. We have to get out of here," Brink said.

Zerie slowly pushed herself up to a sitting position. The top of her head peeked above the broad leaves of the collard greens, so she hunched a bit to keep hidden.

"What do you mean, we need to get out of here?" she asked. "Get out of Pa Underhill's garden?"

"Yes, for starters," Brink replied. "If they've stopped looking for us in the woods, they'll probably start trying to figure out where else we could have gone. And this place is a pretty obvious choice."

"So you think they're hunting for us?" Vashti asked. "Do you think Tabitha told them we were with her?"

"She didn't have to. They saw us," Zerie said. Everything that had happened in the woods was coming into focus now that the immediate danger had passed. "One of the Monkeys landed right between us, Vash. He saw us both."

"And then something roared," Vashti said, nodding. "What was that? Was it a Monkey?"

Zerie shook her head. "I don't know what it was,

but it scared the Monkeys as much as it scared us," she said.

A strange sound echoed through the garden. Vashti gasped, and Zerie fell silent, listening. It was a quiet sound, and in any other circumstance she would have said it sounded like laughter. But Zerie was too upset to even imagine anyone laughing.

"It's stopped," Brink said a moment later. "Do you see anything?"

"No," Zerie answered. "But now I really do want to get out of this garden."

"To go where?" Vashti asked. "We can't go home. If the Winged Monkeys are looking for us, they'll go to our houses." She wrapped her arms around herself. "We can't go home ever again."

Zerie felt as if her entire body had been submerged in ice water.

Never go home again?

Never see her little bedroom or hear the willow scratching at the window?

Never smell Grammy's cooking or feel her warm embrace?

Never gossip with Zelzah or pick apples with Zepho?

"Or we can turn ourselves in," Brink said. "If we let the Monkeys bring us to the Emerald City and Ozma takes our magic away, I'm sure they'll let us go home afterward."

Zerie narrowed her eyes, studying his face. He'd said himself that somebody had told the Winged Monkeys where to find them in the forest. And the only people who had known were him and Vashti and Tabitha.

From the second he'd shown up in the woods, Zerie had suspected that Brink might be a spy, and now here he was trying to talk them into turning themselves in.

"I'm not doing that," she said defiantly. "My magical talent is mine, and no one has the right to take it from me."

"Even if it means leaving home?" Vashti asked. "Living in hiding forever? Knowing that the Monkeys are looking for you?"

"Even then," Zerie said with a lot more certainty than she felt.

"Oh, I'm glad to hear you say that," Brink said, a smile breaking across his face. "I completely agree."

"Then why did you say we should turn ourselves in?" Zerie cried, exasperated.

"I didn't say we should, I said we could. I didn't want to keep you girls from having a chance to stay with your families, if that's what you wanted," Brink replied.

"So those are our only choices?" Vashti asked. "We lose our magic or we lose our families?"

"Yes," Brink said.

"No," said another voice. "There is a third option."

"Who said that?" Zerie cried.

"I did, of course." Zerie blinked to make sure she wasn't imagining things. It was a cat, but such a cat as she had never seen before. This cat was entirely transparent—she could see right through it, straight to its ruby-red heart. The small creature wound its way through the collard stalks, rubbing against each one as it walked.

"You're the Glass Cat," Vashti breathed. "Ozma's cat."

"I beg your pardon, I am nobody's cat," the cat said with a sniff. "Except my own, of course. Cats belong to themselves."

"But you're friends with Princess Ozma. Tabitha told us stories about you." Zerie could hardly take her eyes off the strange creature. "And if you're friends with Ozma, that means you're here to capture us, aren't you?"

"Don't be ridiculous. Why would I have helped you escape from the Winged Monkeys if I wanted you to be caught?" The cat turned her back on Zerie, sat down, and began licking her glass paws.

"You helped us escape? How?" Brink sounded amused.

"I roared, of course. Who did you think it was?"

"You mean that sound? That incredibly loud sound?" Zerie said. "That was you?"

"Cats don't roar," Vashti pointed out. "Cats meow."

The Glass Cat looked sideways at her. "Only cats with no imagination. I don't see any difference between myself and a lion. Except that I'm prettier."

She was pretty, Zerie had to admit. The glass of the cat's body caught the moonlight filtering through the leaves and made her sparkle.

"I don't understand," Zerie said.

"The Winged Monkeys are noisy and rude," the cat said. "And they smell. I like to scare them."

"Okay, but what were you doing in the forest if you weren't spying on us?" Zerie asked.

"Oh, I was spying on you, just not for Ozma," the

cat replied. "I knew you were doing magic, so I came to see it. I can sense magic, you know. I'm a cat."

Brink shot Zerie a skeptical look. "Cats can't sense magic," he said.

"You all seem to know a lot about what cats can and can't do," the cat said. She stood up and stalked off through the plants, her glass tail waving high over her back.

"Great, now she's offended," Vashti said. "Wait! Kitty! You said we had a third option. What does that mean?"

The Glass Cat stopped and glanced over her shoulder. "Never call me Kitty again."

"I won't," Vashti promised. "Sorry."

"Then I'll tell you. You can go home and be caught by the smelly Monkeys. You can flee right now and try to find someplace to hide for the rest of your lives." The cat turned around and stared at them all head-on. "Or you can journey to see Glinda the Good."

"Glinda?" Zerie repeated. "Why would we go to her?"

"You are three witches on your own, and you're not very strong with your talents yet," the cat said.

"We're not witches!" Brink protested.

The cat stared at him with her emerald eyes, not blinking.

"Sorry," Brink said. "I won't interrupt again."

"Glinda is the most powerful sorceress in the Land of Oz. She has the strength to fight Ozma," the cat went on. "If you tell her your story—that you are being hunted like criminals simply for using magic— perhaps Glinda will take your side."

"You mean . . . we should ask Glinda to go to war with Princess Ozma?" Zerie's voice shook as she spoke. "I don't want to do that."

"Glinda won't fight with Ozma. She's Glinda the Good," Vashti said. "Anyway, Glinda is still allowed to use magic. Ozma's ban on magic doesn't apply to Glinda or the Wizard."

"It's precisely because she's good that I expect Glinda will help you," the Glass Cat said. "All good creatures oppose this ban on magic, or they would if they had any brains. Why do you think I'm out here in the middle of nowhere instead of in the Emerald City?"

"Honestly, I have no idea," Zerie said. "I find you very confusing."

"I left Ozma's palace the day she announced her

ban on magic, and I haven't been back since," the Glass Cat said. "I am extremely angry with the princess."

"You've been gone a long time," Vashti said.

"Until Ozma comes to her senses, I won't go back," the cat said. "Imagine if the ban had been in place when I was made! Before I was brought to life, I was nothing but a spun-glass ornament. Without magic, I wouldn't be the beautiful and intelligent feline you see before you."

"We all agree with you that the ban isn't fair," Brink said. "But do you really think Glinda would fight the ruler of Oz?"

"Glinda is Princess Ozma's most important advisor. If you can convince Glinda that the ban must be ended, then she can convince Ozma." The cat lay down and curled itself into a ball. "It's your only chance if you ever want to save your friend," she said, yawning.

"Tabitha? You think Glinda will help Tabitha?" Zerie asked. But the cat was asleep.

"I don't know about this," Vashti said. "First of all, Glinda lives really far away. And second, we have no real reason to think she'll help us."

"But we don't know that she won't," Brink replied.

"It's entirely possible that Glinda isn't aware that the Winged Monkeys are hunting down witches."

"You said we're not witches," Zerie pointed out.

Brink shrugged. "What are we, then?"

Zerie didn't have an answer.

"Do you . . . do you really think she could save Tabitha?" Vashti asked.

"Well, we can't," Zerie said. "We can't fly, and our magic isn't strong enough to fight the Monkeys. But Glinda's is."

"We have to decide now," Brink said. "The longer we stay here, the more likely it is that they'll find us. Are we turning ourselves in, or running away, or going to Glinda?"

Zerie forced herself to think. It was hard to push down the fear in her belly and the despair she felt at the idea of never seeing her family again. But she knew Brink was right—she had to decide. "I hate this," she muttered. "I just wanted everything to go back to normal after yesterday, and instead it got even crazier."

"Well, I'm going to Glinda," Vashti announced. "It's the only way there's any hope, for us or for Tabitha."

"I am, too," Brink said. "I'd rather fight the magic ban than let it destroy my life."

Zerie looked at her friends, crouched in a garden with wide, scared eyes. They were being brave and making a bold choice.

It would be easier to go to the Monkeys and turn themselves over. At least they wouldn't have to sneak around anymore, and maybe once they entered the Forbidden Fountain, they wouldn't even remember what it was like to have a magical talent.

Maybe it wouldn't be so bad. If she chose that, she could be with Tabitha. And afterward, she could come back home and be with Grammy and Mama and Pop. Everything would go back to normal. Normal without magic.

"I always wondered what was down the road of yellow brick," Zerie said. "When I was younger, I would stand there and stare at it."

"Then come with us," Brink told her. "No matter what, nothing will be the same after tonight. You can speed up time, Zerie, but you can't make it go backward."

"Okay." Zerie blinked back tears. "I'll go with you—friends are always strongest together. We'll go to Glinda's palace."

.7.

"The road of yellow brick is to the west of Pa Underhill's house," Vashti said. "So if we go to the right, we can stay under the collard greens for at least half the distance."

"Hang on. We can't just leave right this second," Zerie argued. "I'm wearing my nightgown under this cloak."

Brink and Vashti both looked surprised. "I didn't know about your nighttime magic plans, remember?" Zerie said. "Tabitha snuck in and got me out of bed."

Vashti and Brink were both dressed, since they'd planned to go to the forest behind her back.

"Right." Vashti turned her face away, and all the awkwardness between them suddenly came rushing back to Zerie's mind.

"It's not only you. None of us can leave straight from here," Brink said. "We're going on a long journey. We need supplies. We need food."

"And blankets, I guess," Vashti agreed.

"Something to carry water in. And our sturdiest shoes," Zerie said. "We'll be doing a lot of walking."

"How can we go back to our houses, though?" Vashti asked. "The Monkeys will be looking for us there."

"It was dark out," Brink replied. "They didn't see our faces. They don't know who we are."

"Unless someone told them. The same someone who told them we'd be in the woods," Zerie pointed out.

Vashti stuck her head up over the big leaves. "The airship is still there, but I don't see any Winged Monkeys out in the sky, and the houses in the village are all dark. It doesn't seem as though anybody is awake."

"We have to chance it," Zerie said. "We can't run off with no food or water. We'll just have to get home, pack our things, and get on the road as quickly as possible—before the Monkeys figure out who we are."

"Will Tabitha tell them our names?" Brink asked.

"No!" Zerie snapped. How dare he even ask such a thing? "Tabitha would never betray us."

"Okay, sorry," he mumbled. "I don't know her as well as you do."

None of us know you very well, Zerie thought. Even though she was making plans to escape with Brink, she still didn't entirely trust him. It was weird how you could live near somebody your whole life and not really know much about them.

"We should pick a place to meet up. Somewhere near the road of yellow brick," Zerie said.

"How about behind the old beehive?" Vashti suggested. "It's right at the end of the path that leads to the road."

Zerie nodded. The beehive wasn't a real beehive, it was a statue that someone had made so long ago that nobody in town knew when it had happened. In fact, none of them knew for sure that it was supposed to be a beehive. Personally, Zerie thought it resembled a cyclone. She'd always wondered if it had anything to do with the famous explorer, Dorothy of Kansas.

"I'm going," Vashti said. "If I think about it too long I'll chicken out." She stood up and stalked off toward her house.

"Zerie. Move fast, and be careful," Brink said. Then he took off running.

Move fast, Zerie thought, suddenly realizing that this would be easier for her than for her friends. With her talent, she'd be able to get home and pack her things before the other two had even reached their houses. She could use the extra time to write a note to Grammy.

As she hurried through the garden toward her house, though, she couldn't think of a thing to say to her grandmother. She wanted to explain why she was leaving, but Grammy would already understand. She wanted to apologize for not saying goodbye, but as soon as Grammy saw the Winged Monkeys, she would realize why saying goodbye was impossible. She wanted to say where she was going, but if Ozma's troops saw the note, the whole plan would be ruined.

Before she knew it, Zerie was standing next to her bed, fully dressed, with her bag on her back. She stood still and gazed around her room. Until today, her whole world had been as small as this little room—it held everything she loved, all her trinkets to remind her of her family and her friends. All her dolls from when she was little. All her favorite books and paintings. All her memories.

Now the world felt big and terrifying. Tabitha was gone, and if Zerie stayed here in her room, she would be found and taken, too. Even if she hid under the covers, she wouldn't be safe at home. Not ever again.

Slowly, she snuck into her grandmother's room. Grammy lay sleeping under her quilt, snoring gently. "Goodbye," Zerie whispered. She kissed Grammy's cheek as lightly as she could, making sure not to wake her.

Back downstairs to the kitchen to pack some food. This part Zerie did quickly—as quickly as her talent could manage. Who knew how long it would be before the Winged Monkeys started busting down doors?

Stepping outside, she closed the front door behind her and made a wish that it wouldn't be the last time. Surely she would manage to make it home again someday, wouldn't she?

Zerie closed her eyes and pictured the path to the old beehive . . . and then she was there. She didn't know how fast she'd been moving, but she was definitely at the statue before her friends. The place was deserted.

Or maybe they got caught, she thought, frightened. It was so dark. The beehive was at least six feet tall, and hiding behind it meant that she was in the even-darker shadow cast by the moonlight. Zerie's mind was working feverishly, and she wondered how she would even know if Vashti or Brink had been taken.

Something blotted out the moon, and Zerie's hiding place became pitch black.

She pressed herself up against the beehive and gazed up. There, against the stars, was another airship. It had no lights, and it seemed to draw the darkness of the night into itself, becoming a terrifying void in the sky. The ship moved silently, floating over the village until it stopped over Brink's house.

"Oh, no," Zerie whispered, her heart slamming against her ribcage in fear. "No, no, no."

"What's wrong?"

Brink's voice was so close behind her that Zerie jumped. She spun around to find him only a foot away, his sandy hair sticking out in about ten different directions.

"Don't sneak up on me like that!" Zerie snapped.

"Sorry, I wanted to be quiet." Brink peered over Zerie's shoulder at the new airship. "There's another one?"

"Yes. And it's over your house." Zerie put her hand on his arm. "I'm sorry."

"It's okay. I got everything I need. No one else in my family has magic. They'll be all right," Brink said in a rush.

Zerie knew he was trying to be brave. She could see the worry on his face.

"If Vashti doesn't come soon, I think I might faint," Zerie said. "The Winged Monkeys must know who we are now, if they're over your house. We have to leave right away."

"They're not over Vashti's house," Brink said. "She can still make it."

"Brink, look." Zerie pointed to a spot in the skyway on the far edge of town, over the Pickles' farm. "Is that a cloud?"

He squinted at the dark shape. "No, it's another airship," he said, but Zerie already knew that. "That makes three ships. What are they doing?"

"They can't need three ships to look for us," Zerie

said. "How many Winged Monkeys are they going to send after a few kids? This is crazy."

"I'm here!" Vashti came running up the narrow pathway that led out of the village. "I'm sorry it took so long. There were Monkeys in your family's orchard, Zerie. I had to circle around through Pa Underhill's again to get here."

"They're at my house?" Tears sprang to Zerie's eyes.

"We have to go," Brink said. "Right now." He pointed up. Another ship had appeared straight above them.

"Monkeys!" Vashti gasped as a door opened in the bottom of the airship. Zerie saw a square patch of light, and three dark figures silhouetted against it. Then they were flying, wings beating the air, bodies dropping quickly toward the ground.

"Run," Zerie yelled. She took off as fast as she could—and suddenly remembered that her friends couldn't move as quickly. Zerie forced herself to slow just as she reached the point where the path met up with the road of yellow brick.

A Winged Monkey stood in her way.

Zerie spun around and ran as quickly as she could

back in the other direction, until she reached Vashti and Brink. "The way is blocked. There's a Monkey on the road," she blurted out. "He saw me!"

"They're everywhere." Brink's voice was shaking. "Look! They're surrounding the whole village. Every one of the ships is sending out Monkeys in a big circle around the town."

"We can't get out. We're inside that circle," Vashti cried. "We're trapped."

A screech came from the darkness on the other side of the beehive. It was the Winged Monkey Zerie had seen on the road. It had followed her, and now she'd led it right to her friends.

"I'm sorry," Zerie said. "I'm so sorry, I should've run someplace else so you could get past. I didn't think it through."

"Zerie?" Brink asked suddenly. "Where did you go?"

"I'm right here," she replied, backing away from the Monkey. It wasn't flying. It was walking toward them, a spear in its hands.

"I hear you, but I can't see you," Brink said.

"Me neither," Vashti added. Then she vanished.

"Vash!" Zerie gasped. "You're gone."

"What? No I'm not," Vashti's voice said.

"You're both gone!" Brink cried. "What's happening?"

Zerie looked down at her hands, and saw nothing but the reddish dirt beneath her.

Her feet, her legs, her entire body—all had vanished.

"It's Tabitha!" Zerie said, suddenly understanding. "Tabitha's making us invisible! She's been practicing so much, and tonight she made a nightdrop invisible. She's figured out how to do it. They've got her up in one of these ships, but she's still using her magic. She's using it more than ever before. Good for her!"

"But what about Brink?" Vashti cried.

Zerie's gaze snapped back to Brink. He was still visible, backing away from the terrifying Monkey. The huge dark creature let out a shriek and raised its spear, speeding up as it closed in on Brink.

"Brink, run!" Zerie cried. The Monkey immediately swung around, waving his spear in the direction of her voice. Zerie leaped away from the sharp tip, her breath catching in her throat. The Monkey stood still for a moment, its nostrils twitching as if it could smell her. But its brow was furrowed in confusion.

It can't see me, she thought, trying to calm her fear.

It can't see me. Still, she didn't dare to move again until the Monkey finally turned back toward Brink.

Zerie's heart sank when she saw that Brink was still visible. He raced toward the road, and the Monkey ran after him, its wings unfurling to take off into the sky. If it flew, it would catch up to Brink in a matter of seconds.

Zerie rushed after them, not even sure what she would do when she got there.

"Why isn't Tabitha making him disappear?" Vashti's voice cried from somewhere nearby.

"Maybe she's not strong enough. I can't believe she's even doing this much," Zerie panted.

The Monkey's wings caught the wind, and it rose into the air.

"No!" Zerie moaned as its huge feet left the ground. "No, no, no!"

The creature was flying now, overtaking Brink almost instantly. It loomed over him, impossibly big and frightening.

Zerie watched helplessly as Brink turned to face the Monkey, raising his arm to fend off the spear . . .

And then he vanished.

With a shriek of anger, the Monkey plummeted to

the ground, pouncing on the spot where Brink had been.

Zerie held her breath.

The Monkey hit the dirt and stumbled. It thrashed around violently, trying to connect with its invisible foe, but there was no sound from Brink, and the Monkey's muscular arms didn't touch a thing.

Brink had gotten away.

Relieved, Zerie sank to her knees and tried to calm down. As long as they were quiet and they all stayed far enough away, the Monkey couldn't catch them.

After another minute or two, the Winged Monkey gave an infuriated shriek and took off into the air.

"He's going back to the ship for help," Brink's voice came from the darkness. "We have to get out of here."

"But I can't see you two," Vashti's voice said. "How will we stay together?"

Zerie squinted into the dark. She thought she saw the grass bending about three feet away, and she reached out in that direction, hoping to find her friend.

"Is that you, Zerie?" Brink's voice asked as she felt her arm connect with something. Embarrassed, she snatched her hand away. "Yes, sorry."

"If we can't see one another, we can't stay together," Brink said.

"Then let's all just go, get to the road of yellow brick. Get outside the circle of soldiers," Zerie suggested. "We'll meet up at the first sycamore tree we can find on the left side of the road. There's got to be one somewhere."

"Hurry, before Tabitha gets tired," Brink's voice called. "Good luck!"

I wish I could see Vashti, Zerie thought. *I wish Tabitha were with us, like she should be.* She held her hand up in front of her, but she couldn't see it.

Zerie smiled. Tabitha was with them. She was helping, even when she had no hope left for herself. "Friends are always strongest together," Zerie whispered.

Then she ran, fast as magic, to the road of yellow brick.

.8.

The sun was low in the sky when Zerie woke up, and the air smelled like bread. Or muffins. Or maybe it was cookies? Zerie couldn't quite tell what Grammy was baking, but it was definitely going to be delicious.

"Grammy," she cried, sitting up quickly.

But she wasn't at home, of course.

Vashti lay curled up next to her on the grass, and Brink's satchel was nearby, though Zerie couldn't see him anywhere. A tall, oddly shaped tree loomed over her, its branches heavy with circular fruit.

Zerie sighed. That smell wasn't Grammy's baking, because Grammy was nowhere near here. In fact, Zerie wasn't even sure where here was. The events of the night before were lost in a haze of fear and confusion and exhaustion.

After they'd escaped from the Winged Monkeys, Zerie had met up with Brink and Vashti at the first sycamore she could find along the road of yellow brick. They were all visible again by that time, which had made Vashti sad—it meant that they were too far from Tabitha for her magic to reach them.

Zerie remembered the way the airships had looked from a distance, hovering over her little village like a bank of terrible storm clouds. She'd never felt so scared. The three of them had left the road and run until they couldn't run anymore. Then they had huddled under the tree and fallen asleep.

Vashti yawned, sitting up. "I'm still tired," she said.

"We were awake all night," Zerie pointed out. "Plus, we were running."

"But it must be late in the afternoon by now—look how far down in the sky the sun is. Did we sleep the whole day?" Vashti frowned. "That's not good. The Winged Monkeys will have had time to catch up to us."

"I know. Let's hope they didn't know which way we went," Zerie said. "I don't know where Brink is."

"I don't know where we are," Vashti said. "What's that smell? It's making me hungry."

"It's the town right over that ridge, inside the little forest," Brink replied, appearing over a little hill. "I went to check. The whole place is made of food."

"Food?" Zerie asked. She stood up and went over to examine one of the round fruits on the tree. It had a circle in the middle and white icing on the outside. "It's a doughnut! This is a doughdera tree!" She pulled the doughnut off and took a bite.

"I've heard of those. Tabitha had a story about them," Vashti said. "They grow near Bunbury. That must be the town!"

"The houses are made of crackers," Brink said. "And the ground looked like flour instead of dirt."

"I can't believe it," Zerie cried. "Grammy always told me about Bunbury, and now we're actually there. Did you see any of the people? They're made of bread, you know."

"Tabitha said Bunbury is really well hidden, because the townsfolk are so afraid they'll get eaten. So how come we could find it?" Vashti asked.

"Maybe because we were looking for a hiding place, too?" Brink guessed.

"Oh." Vashti's excited smile faltered.

The doughnut suddenly tasted like sawdust in Zerie's mouth. "We should probably stay away from Bunbury, huh?" she asked. "We don't want to lead Ozma's troops to the town."

"The Winged Monkeys aren't going to bother anyone unless they're practicing magic. We wouldn't be a danger to them," Brink replied.

"But they might be a danger to us," Vashti said. "Just because they're pastries doesn't mean they're nice people. If they know we're running from Ozma, they might turn us in."

"I guess that's true." Zerie felt a stab of disappointment. "Still, I'd love to see a person made of food."

"I think Vashti's right," Brink said. "We can't go to Bunbury. We can't go anywhere that people might see us and report us . . . not until we get to Glinda's palace."

"It's not only people who can tell on you." The Glass Cat casually jumped down from a high branch of the doughdera tree as if she'd been a part of the conversation all along. "Ozma has spies everywhere."

"Where did you come from?" Zerie cried. "How did you find us?"

"I'm a cat," said the cat. "I'm naturally the greatest hunter in the world. I can find anyone."

"What do you mean, there are spies everywhere?" Vashti said.

"The Winged Monkeys are big and uncouth. Ozma uses other flying creatures whenever she can. They don't scare people like the monkeys do." The cat sniffed Zerie's doughnut and shuddered.

"You mean like birds?" Brink asked.

"Birds, butterflies, dragonflies, unicornflies . . . even plain old moths," the cat replied. "The clockwork kind. You know about those, Brink, don't you?"

Brink sank down to sit on the grass next to Zerie. "I never did much clockwork. That was Ned's thing. My father tried to teach me to fix regular old clocks, but I didn't even like that."

Zerie noticed that he wouldn't look at her or Vashti when he said his brother's name. She couldn't blame him; she didn't want to meet their eyes, either. "But did Ned make things like that? Flying spies?" she asked.

"I never heard of him doing any work for Ozma," Brink said. "But he sure did like to make birds."

"He made gorgeous birds," Vashti put in. "I saw

him testing a whole flock of rainbow finches one time. They looked just like the real ones."

"The real ones are very stupid. You don't have to worry about them unless you're a worm," the cat said. "It's the clockwork ones who work for Princess Ozma."

Zerie didn't know whether to laugh or not. In fact, she wasn't sure what to think of the Glass Cat in general. She certainly wasn't always nice, even though she sometimes seemed helpful. "And the real butterflies, are they stupid too?" Zerie asked.

"I never talk to bugs. I only eat them," the cat replied. "Though not butterflies, of course. They taste bitter."

"We should go," Brink said, interrupting the odd conversation. "We all slept the whole day away, and now we only have an hour or two before it gets dark."

"Are we taking the road of yellow brick?" Vashti asked. "Is it safe? Ozma's soldiers are probably patrolling it. She has mounted soldiers, not just monkeys. At least that's what Tabitha used to say."

"We have to take the road—how else will we find the palace?" Zerie said. "The road goes straight to it."

"The road is not safe, and you shouldn't take it. I

will guide you to Glinda's Palace," the Glass Cat said. "I was created in that area, and I know the countryside very well."

"Great. Thank you," Brink replied. "Let's go."

"Absolutely not. We won't leave until dark," the cat said. She curled herself into a circle and tucked her nose under her spun-glass tail.

"What are you talking about? We can't travel at night," Vashti protested. "We won't be able to see!"

"I don't know," Zerie said, thinking it through. "She may have a point. During the day, anyone might see us. People are awake, and so are birds and butterflies, and . . . well, we're easier to spot in the daylight."

"Oh, that wasn't my point," the cat said, yawning. "I simply don't do much during the day. I'm nocturnal."

"But you're still right, Zerie. We've already lost today. We might as well travel tonight, since we won't be tired," Brink said. "You're being smart, to think about how visible we are in the sun. We all need to start behaving that way—we need to remember that we are wanted people."

"I don't like that idea," Vashti said quietly.

"None of us do, but it's the truth." Zerie took a deep breath. "We decided to run, not to turn ourselves in. We knew that it meant we were going to be followed by Ozma's troops."

Vashti didn't answer.

"So we'll travel at night and sleep during the day," Brink said. "We should set a watch when we're sleeping. One of us will need to stay awake and make sure nobody finds us. We can take turns."

"Why can't the Glass Cat just keep watch? She doesn't need to sleep at all," Vashti pointed out.

"I most certainly do," the cat said, picking up her head.

"But you're made of glass," Brink said.

"I like to nap." The cat tucked her nose back under her tail and that was that.

Nobody said anything after the cat went to sleep. Zerie thought it felt awkward, but she wasn't sure what to say. She and Vashti had never fought before, and yesterday they'd . . . well, she wasn't sure what it had been. Sort of a fight. Sort of an embarrassing realization that they both liked the same boy. Whatever it was, it felt as if a hundred years had gone by since then. So much had happened that it seemed silly to worry about who had a crush on whom.

If Brink wasn't here, I would just talk to Vashti about

it, Zerie thought. But she couldn't very well discuss Brink's brother in front of him. She figured Vashti probably felt the same way.

"How long will it take to reach Glinda?" she asked, just to have something to say.

"Glinda's palace is at the far south of Quadling Country, that's what Tabitha always said," Vashti replied. "And we're toward the north. So we have to travel the whole length of Quadling Country."

Just thinking about Tabitha made Zerie sad. She could hardly bear to think of what her friend must be going through right this minute. Was she imprisoned in the airship, alone and afraid? Had the Winged Monkeys taken her to the Emerald City yet? Or were they still hovering over the village, looking for Tabitha's friends?

Zerie shivered, though it wasn't very cold. Their only hope to help Tabitha was to get Glinda on their side.

"I can't believe we're going to see Glinda the Good," Zerie said. "That's not something normal people do. Will she even let us in? I mean, we're nobodies."

"The Glass Cat thinks she will, and she knows Glinda," Brink replied. "I guess we have to trust her."

"I wish Tabitha was here. She's the one who would love to meet Glinda," Vashti said.

Zerie nodded sadly. "She always wanted to meet all the famous people. I always just wanted to see the Land of Oz."

"Well, you're going to get your wish," Brink said. "We have a lot of walking through Oz to do before we reach Glinda. And we're going to need our magic. We should practice."

Vashti looked startled. "Why would we need magic? That's the last thing we should do! What about all those birds and butterflies and other clockwork spies the cat talked about?"

"We need magic to get away from them," Brink said. He turned to Zerie. "Did you use your talent to help you escape last night?"

"Yes," she replied. "I moved fast with my magic, and I got away from my house before Ozma's troops got there. Did you use yours?"

Brink nodded. "There was a Winged Monkey on my front porch when I wanted to leave. I made an illusion of the door being closed. Then I opened the real door and slipped out without him noticing. I man-aged to hold the illusion until I was halfway to the old beehive," he said proudly. "I've never done anything like that before."

"I don't think I would've gotten away in time without my talent," Zerie said. "You're right, Brink, we probably will need it on the journey. Who knows what might happen?"

Vashti shook her head. "You two have useful talents. Levitation won't help me escape from Ozma's spies."

Zerie tried to think of a way that her friend's talent would help, but she couldn't come up with one. "You should still practice, just in case. Try to levitate something big," she suggested.

"I don't want to. I'm going to sleep some more before we have to travel tonight," Vashti said. She lay back down on the grass and turned her back to them.

Zerie and Brink exchanged glances. He shrugged, picked a doughnut from the tree, and held it out to her. "Can you speed it up? Make it grow old?"

"An old doughnut? Why?" Zerie wrinkled her nose.

"It's what we were working on when the Monkeys caught us. You were speeding up the nightdrop. So now speed up the doughnut. Now that I've picked it, it won't stay fresh. It will turn stale eventually . . . so speed it up until it does."

Zerie gazed at the moist, yummy pastry and thought about how it would age—first hardening ever so slightly, then drying up, the icing becoming more solid and starting to crack, and finally becoming hard and dead like a rock. That's when the mold would begin to grow, its greenish-black fuzziness spreading slowly over the entire doughnut like a disease. She closed her eyes and pictured it happening.

Somehow she knew when it was done. It felt as if a burst of strength had left her body, and she was certain that the magic was complete.

When her eyes opened, Brink was making a disgusted face at the moldy, smelly pastry in his hand. Holding it gingerly between two fingers, he tossed it as far away as he could. "See? Now you know how to speed up a life cycle," Brink told her. "There's more to you than just running fast, Zerie Greenapple."

.9.

"What's that really dark thing?" Zerie asked the Glass Cat later that night.

They'd been walking for several hours, ever since the sun went down. Bunbury was far behind them, and now they were crossing a small river by jumping from one bright red river rock to the next.

The cat had said that the farther south they went in Quadling Country, the redder the landscape would get. Zerie paused and pointed toward the horizon, where a reddish-black ridge stood out against the sky.

"It's Big Enough Mountain," the cat said, flicking

her tail as she leaped from the final rock onto the shore. "Obviously."

Brink shot Zerie a smile, and she smiled back. She was starting to get used to the cat's prickly personality. Zelzah's kitty back home didn't talk, but if he could have, he would probably be just as snooty as the Glass Cat.

"Tabitha once said that a giant lived on Big Enough Mountain," Vashti commented as they started off across a dark meadow. "Is that true?"

"Of course it's true. His name is Loxo. But he's not a giant anymore," the cat replied. "He's just a regular boring person like the rest of you."

"Do we have to climb over the mountain?" Brink asked. "Or can we go around?"

"We'll go around it," the cat said. "We just have to be careful of the Foot Hills."

"Why? What could happen in the Foot Hills?" Zerie asked.

"They're Foot Hills. They might—" Whatever the cat had been about to say was drowned out by a gigantic thump.

The Glass Cat took off running. Zerie, Brink, and Vashti looked at one another in confusion.

Thump.

Dirt, grass, and rock shot into the air as if someone had dropped a heavy boulder and displaced the earth to their left.

Thump.

This time the sound was deafening, and the spray of debris was only two feet away.

Zerie looked up. A humongous dark-brown foot hung in the air over her head.

"Watch out!" she screamed, pushing Brink and Vashti out of the way—just as the huge foot smashed onto the ground where they'd been standing. Dirt and grass kicked up from the impact, and Zerie couldn't help thinking about how everything underneath that foot must have been flattened.

"There's another one!" Brink yelled, pointing to the right. He grabbed Zerie's hand and yanked her to her feet. "Run."

Zerie took a step—*thump.* Another gigantic foot hit the ground in front of her. "How many of these things are there?" she cried.

"A lot." Vashti's voice shook as she pointed toward Big Enough Mountain. "They're everywhere."

Zerie raised her eyes toward the mountain.

Everything in between here and there, every bit of land, was moving. It was walking. The land itself had taken the form of feet—huge reddish feet covered in dirt and pebbles and bits of grass. But the feet themselves weren't made of dirt. Seeing them from a distance, stamping down everything in their path, Zerie could see that these feet were solid rock. "They're granite, like the mountain," she whispered. "Look at the footprints."

"Each print is so deep," Vashti said. "Those feet are incredibly heavy."

"They're the Foot Hills," Brink put in. "The foothills of a mountain are made of the same rock as the mountain. These ones are the same as Big Enough Mountain."

"Except they're walking," Zerie cried. She yanked her friends backward just as another foot slammed into the earth in front of them. "We have to get out of here before we get crushed."

"Which way did the cat go?" Brink asked.

Zerie looked around wildly. "I don't know! All the jumping away from the Foot Hills has me completely turned around."

"The mountain was a little to the right when we

heard the first foot. So they've been herding us closer to it, because now it's in right in front of us," Vashti said.

"So we have to go back that way. To the left," Zerie said, just before the next foot came down.

Thump.

"Are they trying to step on us?" Brink cried after they'd all jumped out of the way. Zerie noticed that his chest was heaving. He was out of breath from avoiding the Foot Hills. So was Vashti—her eyes were wide and frightened, and Zerie saw sweat on her brow.

But Zerie felt fine. Scared, but fine. Her heartbeat was steady, and her breathing came easy. *I guess I'm used to moving fast, so my body doesn't get as tired*, she thought.

Another foot slammed down. They all leaped to the right to get away from it, but the foot landed on the hem of Brink's pant leg. He jerked it free, tearing the fabric.

"We have to go left," Vashti said, panting.

This is bad. They're getting too worn out to move away from the Foot Hills. They're going to get stepped on, Zerie thought. If only her friends had her talent, they wouldn't be so exhausted.

"I wish you had my talent," she blurted out. Vashti and Brink both stared at her.

Thump.

Another footstep shook the ground a few feet away. The vibrations were so strong that Vashti lost her balance. Brink caught her before she fell, but it was clear they couldn't last much longer.

"My talent!" Zerie cried. She grabbed each of her friends by a hand and ran as fast as she could away from the next giant foot. Vashti and Brink stumbled after her, almost falling.

"You can't do that," Vashti said. "We can't run that fast."

Zerie frowned. Could it be that her talent didn't work if she tried to bring someone else along? But that didn't make sense. Grammy always said the reason people had magic was because they were supposed to use it to help others. And friends were strongest together. So maybe she was simply doing it wrong.

When I move fast by myself, I picture the end point of where I want to be, and then I'm there. I don't even notice myself moving, Zerie thought. She peered into the distance, trying to find a landmark in the direction they'd come from. Finally she saw it—a glint of light in the darkness. It was the moon shining on the little river they'd crossed earlier. There hadn't been any huge feet in that river.

Thump.

Vashti screamed as the next foot landed an inch away from her.

Zerie forced herself to ignore her terror. She took hold of Vashti's hand and Brink's. Then she closed her eyes and pictured the path they'd walked from the river. All she had to do was go back that way, through the dark field, to the bright red rocks in the middle of the river. It wasn't far . . .

"Zerie, you did it!" Brink cried.

When she opened her eyes, she saw that all three of them stood on a red rock in the water, just as she'd pictured it. "I did it! I used my talent to help us all," she breathed.

Vashti smiled, her dark eyes filled with relief. "You're a hero, Z," she said.

And then Vashti fell, her foot slipping on the slick rock. She landed with a splash in the river, and the current swept her off toward the far bank. Spluttering and wet, she clambered up onto the shore.

"Vashti, no! Not on that side!" Zerie yelled.

But her friend was too far away to hear.

"The Foot Hills started almost immediately after we got across the river. They could get her right where she is," Brink said grimly. He jumped into the water and began to swim toward Vashti.

"Now you'll both get smooshed," Zerie called after him. "Vashti! Swim back to the other side! Hurry!" she screamed as loud as she could.

The rushing water carried her voice away.

Brink hadn't reached Vashti yet when the foot appeared. The Foot Hill rose up from the earth, looking like a normal hill, until suddenly the toes appeared at the crest, followed by the long sole and the wide heel. From this distance, Zerie could see that it was about the length of the orchard wagon back home, and as wide as her front porch. Up into the air it rose, higher and higher, until it was almost directly over Vashti.

"Vashti!" Zerie screamed.

But her best friend was busy wringing out her shirt, not even glancing up. She must have thought they'd reached safety.

Brink swam faster, but it was no use. He couldn't

make it in time. Zerie tried to picture herself getting to the far bank, grabbing Vashti, and coming back to this rock. But she was too frantic; she couldn't force herself to imagine the route. Her eyes refused to stop seeing what was happening right in front of her. The Foot Hill was moving down now, and it was going to crush Vashti.

"Age it like the nightdrop," Zerie whispered to herself. "Like the doughnut." She didn't know where the idea came from, and she didn't stop to think about it.

Rock wasn't alive, but it could age. That's what sand was, wasn't it? Rock that had been around for so long that it wore down into a billion tiny pieces.

The Foot Hill is only rock, she thought, staring at it. *Rock turns to sand. This dark rock will be dark sand, sand spilling right here onto the banks of the river. Sand. Sand. Sand.*

And then the dark rock was dark sand.

"Arrghh!" Vashti yelled as a rain of dark sand landed on top of her. There was so much of it that it pushed her to the ground and piled up around her. Brink climbed from the river, grabbed Vashti's arm, and yanked her back into the water. The sand continued to pile up, forming a huge hill where Vashti had been.

Shaking, Zerie sank down onto the slick rock. Her legs felt like noodles, and she thought she might fall if she didn't sit. Her heart hammered in her chest, from terror or relief—she wasn't quite sure which.

Brink and Vashti made it to the other side of the river and clambered up onto the bank. Vashti waved Zerie over, but Zerie felt too exhausted to even step back over the rocks to shore. In fact, she thought she might just sleep right where she was.

Her eyes fluttered closed.

When she opened them again, Brink was carrying her as he hopped from stone to stone back across the river.

Then she was lying on the grass, staring up at the stars, while the thumping of the Foot Hills echoed through the air on the far side of the water.

"She's in shock," Vashti's voice drifted in to her consciousness.

"She used so much magic to explode the Foot Hill. I think she's wiped out," Brink replied. His face came into focus over Zerie's, blocking out the sky. He looked worried.

"Let's find a place where we can hide and Zerie can sleep. It's almost dawn anyway," Vashti said. "We'll have to figure out another way to get to Glinda's Palace tomorrow night. We can't go through the Foot Hills."

Then Brink was carrying her again, and Zerie let the tiredness overtake her. She vaguely knew that they'd crawled into a little abandoned farm shed and that Brink was by the door keeping watch.

And she knew that Vashti was holding her hand as they settled in.

"You saved my life, Zerie," Vashti whispered. "Your talent is amazing. You're my hero."

Whatever weirdness had been between them was gone. Zerie smiled and went to sleep.

.10.

A strange sound woke Zerie. Something vibrated on her feet, and she sat up quickly, confused.

The Glass Cat lay on top of Zerie's feet, purring with her eyes closed.

"When did you come back?" Zerie asked grumpily. She hadn't forgiven the cat for taking off at the first sign of the terrifying Foot Hills. Or, for that matter, for not telling them about the giant feet in the first place.

The cat yawned, turned on her side, and kept right on sleeping and purring.

"She showed up about two hours ago," Brink said. "She seemed surprised that we'd managed to survive the Foot Hills, and then she lay down for a nap."

Zerie yawned, too. It was already getting dark. Vashti snored softly on the floor beside her. "Did I sleep all day?" she asked Brink. "Wait. Were you on watch all day? You're supposed to wake one of us up to take over when you get tired."

Brink shrugged, his cheeks flushing. "The two of you had a tough time last night. Vashti almost got killed, and you saved her. Well, first you saved all of us and then you saved her. I figure you're pretty tired."

"You went swimming in the river and jumped away from all those big feet. You must be tired, too," Zerie pointed out.

"I can take it," Brink said. He didn't sound as if he was boasting. Zerie knew he was simply being honest.

"Thank you," she told him. "That was really sweet."

The red of his cheeks deepened. "I guess we have to figure out what to do now, huh?"

Zerie said, "I'm not going anywhere near those Foot Hills again. There must be a different way to Glinda's Palace."

"Maybe we should go back to the road," Brink suggested. "The road of yellow brick leads straight there."

"But Ozma's spies will be watching it, remember?" Zerie frowned. "At least we thought they would be. I guess we could give it a try. It's been two days since we ran away, and they might not even know which direction we went in."

"There are enough Winged Monkeys to watch the whole of Oz," the cat said without even opening her eyes. "And you're forgetting Ozma's regular soldiers— with their horses, they can patrol the length of road from Glinda to the Emerald City in just one day."

"Do you really think Ozma will spend that much energy trying to find us?" Zerie asked. "We're only three little people. We're not dangerous."

The Glass Cat didn't answer. She seemed to be asleep again.

"I say we risk it," Brink said. "If it's the road or the Foot Hills, we'll be in danger either way."

"What are we risking?" Vashti asked, sitting up.

"It will be dark soon. Brink and I thought maybe we should take the road of yellow brick," Zerie said. "At night, it won't be so easy for spies to see us. And at least we won't get stomped on."

"Sounds okay to me." Vashti shuddered. "Those feet were horrible. I'm not sure it's worth it to keep my talent if it means getting killed."

"Don't say that," Zerie said with a gasp. "Of course

it's worth it! It's not right that we shouldn't use the magic we were born with, and it's not right that the Winged Monkeys can just come and take Tabitha away. We'll get to Glinda, and she'll help us, and then it will be perfectly legal to have a talent like yours. And who knows? Maybe she can prevent Ozma from taking Tabitha's talent away."

"It's easy for you to think that way. Your talent is amazing," Vashti replied. "You used it to save me—and that makes it important. Tabitha, too—she saved us from the airship. My talent doesn't help anyone."

Zerie didn't know what to say. She tried again to think of a way that levitating something would be helpful, but she couldn't come up with one.

"All magic is there to help people. That's why it exists," Brink said. "Just because you haven't figured out how yet doesn't mean your talent is worthless, Vashti."

Vashti smiled at him, and Zerie shot him a grateful look. He'd managed to cheer Vashti up when Zerie couldn't. In fact, now that she thought about it, Brink always seemed to be cheerful. She hadn't liked the idea of running away with him or traveling so far together, but Brink was turning out to be very helpful.

When Vashti snuck out to get a drink from the well in the field behind them, Zerie decided to stay with Brink. She figured he would feel more like they were friends if she stopped treating him like a tagalong.

As soon as the sun set, the three friends left their shelter and headed across the fields toward the road of yellow brick. It took them half an hour of arguing with the Glass Cat before she would agree to guide them to the road, and even as they made their way toward it, her spun-glass tail still switched angrily.

"I don't know what she's so upset about. She'll just run off again if there's any trouble," Zerie murmured to Vashti.

Vashti giggled. "Did she ever explain herself?"

"Brink says she thought the Foot Hills usually stay closer to Big Enough Mountain," Zerie replied. "He said she seemed pretty offended that they'd moved."

"Everything seems to offend her," Vashti said.

"She told Brink that cats are intelligent enough to run when they sense danger," Zerie said. "And that they're fast enough to get away from almost anything."

"If only they were loyal enough to bring their friends with them," Vashti murmured.

"Cats are solitary creatures," the cat said frostily. "And by the way, we have excellent hearing."

Vashti and Zerie exchanged an embarrassed look, and Zerie laughed.

"There's the road!" Brink cried, pointing up ahead to where a faint golden line snaked through the darkness. "Let's go!"

"Hold on," Zerie said. "We need to sneak up on it. We all have to stay quiet and keep a watch for soldiers, or birds, or flying clockworks."

The Glass Cat snorted. "You'll never see Ozma's spies. You're just silly children, while they are royal observers. As soon as you set foot on the road, you're doomed."

"Why are you coming with us, then?" Vashti asked.

The cat didn't answer. She just stalked toward the road, tail held high.

Hiding in the low, thick bushes that lined this part of the road, Zerie peered straight across the interwoven bricks. They were so yellow that they gave off a soft glow even at night, and so evenly placed and smooth that there were no crevices for small spies to hide in. Zerie would've been able to see the smallest chipmunk or snail on the road. She saw nothing.

"Nobody coming from the left," Brink reported from beside her.

"No one on the right, either," Vashti whispered.

"And nothing on the other side, though it looks like there might be a drop-off over there," Zerie said.

"If we're going to chance it, we need to walk as fast as we can and as silently as we can," Brink said. "We'll all have to act like the Glass Cat."

The cat's emerald eyes glittered a bit in the moonlight as she turned to look at him. "That's right," she said, a little less snippily than before.

Brink even manages to make nice with the Glass Cat, Zerie thought. *I didn't think anybody could do that.*

"Here we go," Vashti said. She reached for Zerie's hand, and Zerie grabbed onto Brink with her other hand.

Together they stepped onto the yellow bricks, and Zerie realized she'd been holding her breath, as if the Winged Monkeys were going to swoop down on them the second they appeared on the road.

The Glass Cat padded softly down the center of the road, and the three friends followed as quickly and quietly as possible. There were no sounds other than the usual crickets and night birds, but even those felt ominous. Zerie found herself looking over her shoulder as she walked, and more than once she caught Brink jumping at a sudden breeze or the hoot of an owl.

"How will we know if a spy has seen us?" Vashti whispered after about half an hour. "Won't it just fly back to Ozma and report? It won't come after us, so how will we know?"

"I'm not sure," Zerie said, fear creeping up her spine. "I guess we won't know until we see an airship."

An ear-splitting scream rang out across the land.

Zerie froze, her friends beside her. For a moment all was silent. And then . . .

Thundering hooves. There was no mistaking the sound.

"Horses!" Vashti gasped. "It must be Ozma's soldiers!"

"Where are they?" Brink asked. "I can't tell if the noise is in front of us or behind us!"

"Get off the road," Zerie cried. The Glass Cat was already running. This time they all took off after her.

"We have to hide," Vashti panted as they raced over the yellow bricks. "But I can't see anything in the dark."

"The cat can. She'll find a place. We just have to follow," Brink replied.

Sure enough, the Glass Cat suddenly veered to the left and leaped off the edge of the road. She vanished into the darkness.

Vashti slowed.

"There's a drop-off on that side, remember?" Zerie said, grabbing her friend's arm. "We have to jump, like the cat. Hurry! The hooves are getting louder!"

"We don't know how far our fall will be," Vashti protested, but she ran along with Zerie anyway.

Brink reached the edge of the road and jumped. Zerie got there a second later.

She wanted to stop and look over. She had no idea if it was two feet or twenty. But the pounding hooves were so loud that the horses had to be almost on top of them. There was no time to hesitate. Clutching Vashti's arm, she plunged over the edge.

"Float," Vashti cried. "Float!"

They crashed into a dense bush and sank between the red leaves. Vashti was crying.

"Hush!" Zerie whispered, stroking her friend's arm. "We can't let them hear us."

The hoofbeats slowed, and then stopped. Zerie

held her breath and peered up into the darkness above the bushes. The branches were enough to hide them from view, she hoped. At least in the darkness. *Can Ozma's spies see in the dark like the cat can?* she wondered. *That would be bad.*

There were some scuffling noises on the road, and then slowly the hoofbeats began again, moving away. Finally, the sound of horses faded into the distance.

Zerie waited for five more minutes before she even moved. "Are you hurt?" she asked, turning to Vashti. "Why were you crying? Did the branches scratch you?"

"No. Well, yes. But not badly." Vashti clambered out of the thick bush, tugging her clothes off the branches. "But I tried to stop our fall. I tried to levitate us." Vashti's words came out as sobs. "It didn't work! We didn't float."

"Oh, Vash." Zerie pulled herself out of the bushes. "I'm sorry. But that was a great idea. Next time it will work."

"You did it when you had to. You saved me," Vashti said.

"Well . . ." Zerie thought about it. "This fall didn't do anything more than knock the breath out of us. We weren't in danger from it, even though we didn't know that. Maybe your talent didn't work because we didn't really need it."

Vashti took a deep breath and swiped at her tears. "I guess we don't know much about how this magic stuff works yet."

"You certainly don't know much about hiding, either," the voice of the Glass Cat said from somewhere in the darkness. "You're both being far too loud."

"Sorry! Where are you?" Zerie asked, lowering her voice.

"Down here," Brink responded. "There's a ditch, and the bushes grow right over it."

"Indeed the undergrowth is dense, but one can hardly call it undergrowth when it grows over one's person, and so we cannot definitively say what it might be that covers this ditch," said a girl's voice.

Vashti and Zerie exchanged confused looks. "Who said that?" Vashti asked.

"Oh! You shouldn't have said anything, not a thing, you should've stayed quiet," cried another voice, this one a boy's. "What if those creatures are unfriendly? What if they throw us out of our hiding place? If they do that, then we have nowhere else to go. If we have nowhere else to go, we'll get caught for sure. If we get caught—"

"Brink?" Zerie interrupted the string of words. "What's going on?"

"Follow my voice," he replied. "When you get to the edge of the ditch, I'll see you and help you climb down."

"Silly people, not knowing how to climb in the dark," the Glass Cat put in.

"Oh!" the strange boy said. "If they fall, they'll get hurt. If they get hurt, they'll need medical attention! If they need medical attention, they'll have to tell others where we're hiding."

"Indubitably, to plummet from a great height can certainly result in injury to the body; however, we know not what type of creature these disembodied voices may be," the girl's voice replied. "Therefore the tumble from above may be either catastrophic or a dud."

"Brink? Are those people with you?" Zerie called as quietly as possible.

"Yes. They are." Brink sounded annoyed.

Zerie inched forward in the direction of the voices,

afraid with every step that she was about to fall again. This land was covered with the same type of low, prickly red bushes she and Vashti had landed in, stretching as far as she could see. "Brink? How did you end up in a ditch?" she called, wanting to hear his voice instead of the strange ones.

"I followed the cat," he called back. "She led me straight to it."

"This is the only place to hide for at least a mile," the Glass Cat said. "Which is why we're stuck hiding here with these loons."

"I don't understand what's going on," Vashti whispered, gripping Zerie's hand.

"Me either. And I can't make out any ditches," Zerie replied.

"I see you!" Brink cried. "Look down."

Zerie did. There, at the base of the closest prickly bush, was a deeper section of darkness, like a hole. And sticking out of the hole was a hand.

Brink.

Dropping to her knees, Zerie peered into the blackness. Brink's face stared back at her. "You're practically underground!" Zerie gasped. "How did you get down there?"

"You just have to push the bushes aside. They're prickly, but they're ticklish," Brink said. "Watch." He ran his fingers up and down the nearest branch, and the bush shivered, shook, and pulled away from him. He did the same thing to the two branches next to it, and they both pulled away as well.

"I wish I'd known that when we were trying to climb out of them before," Vashti said. "One of these things tore my shirt!"

Zerie knelt down and tickled the bushes until there was an opening between the branches big enough to climb through. Everything was darker inside, but Brink was there to help her down. Once she and Vashti were safe inside the ditch, Zerie took a look around.

It was a deep ditch, about six feet from the bottom to the top where the tickle-bushes grew, their long branches intertwining to form a roof over the ditch. The whole thing ran like a tunnel for about twenty feet beneath the bushes, so there was plenty of room for Zerie, her friends, and the two other people huddled in there with them.

One was a boy who looked to be about Ned Springer's age. He had a round face, wore denim overalls and a straw farm hat, and as far as Zerie could see, he could've been a neighbor from their village. The other person was a girl of around the same age. Her hair was long and blond—Zerie could tell because it was light against the darkness. She had her hands on her hips and her eyebrows were drawn together in consternation.

"There can be no doubt that this fine hole in the ground was made to accommodate two people with ample room," the girl said. "One could argue that more than two would fit and still not find themselves forced to occupy so small a space that their comfort would be compromised. However, the amount of space required to satisfy one's personal comfort is a variable and individual issue, and we cannot presume to decide for one another what that amount of space would be, although I find myself in this circumstance inclined to worry about—"

"Worry! You're worried?" the boy said, cutting her off. "Oh, no! What shall we do? If you're worried when you're so sensible, how will I know how to handle it? If you get scared, I'll certainly be even more scared than you, and if I am even more scared, I might begin to scream and tear my way out of this ditch and run onto the road and be caught!"

Zerie stared at them both, baffled.

"What on earth are they talking about?" Vashti asked.

"We are quite obviously having a discussion about multiple layers of the reality in which we find ourselves," the girl replied. "A discussion might take one form when talking about the present and a separate form when discussing the multiple iterations of the future, which as we all know is an unfathomable state that does not allow one to draw any conclusions. Nevertheless, it is the human condition to attempt control of the aforementioned iterations—"

"Stop!" Zerie said, holding up her hand. "I don't care what you're talking about. I want to know who you are."

"Oh!" The girl seemed startled by the question. "I am Ednah Florance, of the Florances of Rigmarole Town, although that is a suffix that we have only recently acquired, and by recently I refer, of course, to the last three generations. So few Rigmaroles are Rigmaroles born; you are familiar, I assume, with the Defensive Settlements of Oz, in which any citizen determined to be a Rigmarole is sent to live in Rigmarole Town? This means by necessity that most

Rigmaroles originate from other geographical areas of the Land of Oz, but the Florances of Rigmarole have been Rigmaroles born for several years and therefore the suffix 'of Rigmarole Town' was adopted to celebrate the distinct strain of Rigmarole culture that we—"

"Okay, great!" Zerie interrupted. "And who are you?" she asked the boy, although she was almost afraid of the answer.

"I'm Edmond," he replied. "Or at least that's what my mother told me my name was. But what if she was wrong? What if she got confused between my brother Edgar and myself? What if I'm truly Edgar and not Edmond? That would mean that I've been acting like an Edmond when I should be acting like an Edgar, and who knows what an Edgar would've done in our situation? What I mean is, what if—"

His voice became higher and higher as he went on, and Zerie got the feeling he would keep spinning out what-ifs for as long as they let him talk.

"Your situation?" she cut in. "What situation?"

For a moment both Ednah and Edmond were silent. Zerie could hardly believe it.

"You two are hiding, just like we are," Brink

prompted them. "You were here already when I followed the cat down into the ditch. So tell us, why are Ozma's soldiers after you?"

"Ozma's soldiers!" Edmond practically shrieked. "Princess Ozma is hunting us down? What if she finds us? If she finds us we'll be dragged in front of her, and if we're dragged in front of her I'll be terrified by her power and beauty, and if I'm terrified—"

"Edmond, calm your pounding heart and your speeding pulse and your irrational fear-spinning, if you're able," Ednah said, taking his hand. "Though, to be fair, I am also filled with an unaccountable terror at the implication that the military might of the ruler of the Land of Oz would be brought to bear against us for so minor a crime that—"

"What are you talking about?" Vashti demanded loudly.

"Ssshhhh!" everyone in the ditch told her.

"Cease and desist from asking them questions immediately!" the Glass Cat said. "The Rigmarole will never stop talking, but will never actually get to the point. And the Flutterbudget will keep spouting unlikely possibilities until the sun comes up."

"Are you the Flutterbudget?" Brink asked Edmond.

"What did I just say?" cried the Glass Cat, before Edmond could answer.

"Sorry," Brink muttered.

"You're holding hands," Zerie commented, studying Ednah and Edmond in the dim light. "Are you together?"

"Most assuredly we are together in that we occupy the same general space at the same general time, which is—"

"She means are you a couple," Vashti interrupted before Ednah could continue. "Just nod or shake your heads no."

They both nodded.

"That's preposterous," the Glass Cat said. "Rigmaroles stay in Rigmarole Town by law, expressly so that they won't torture other people with their constant speechifying. And Flutterbudgets live in Flutterbudget Center for the same reason. Neither one of you should have left home, and the two of you should never have met, and every conversation you have with one another will be utterly inane."

"That doesn't matter if they're in love," Zerie said. "Is that why you're here, so far from your homes? And why you're hiding?"

Ednah and Edmond both opened their mouths to talk. "Nod or shake your heads no!" Vashti reminded them. After a moment, they nodded.

"But why would Ozma's soldiers be looking for a couple in love?" Brink asked. "I know that they're not supposed to leave their towns, but surely it isn't actually against the law?"

"It should be," the cat said.

"Ednah's mother began explaining to my mother why we shouldn't be allowed to date," Edmond said, "and my mother became so frightened of the possibilities that she began wailing and thinking about all the what-ifs, and then Ednah's mother had to explain away every single one of the what-ifs, and after a few days they both fainted from hunger because they'd been talking the entire time. That's why we decided to leave, so we wouldn't put them in any more danger from being together."

"Edmond! That was a very normal explanation!" Zerie cried. "Good for you!"

He began to answer, but she cut him off before he could go into any what-iffing. "So you two are running off to be together. But why are you hiding from the soldiers?"

"We . . ." Ednah paused, clearly trying to think of how to say it. "We . . . aren't." She clapped her hand over her mouth to stop the rest of the words from spilling out.

Brink nudged Zerie and smiled. "You're getting to them! They're starting to talk like regular people," he whispered.

"Then why are you in this ditch?" Vashti asked. "You said you were hiding."

"In fact *you* said we were hiding," Ednah began, "and we never confirmed as much, although we also never denied as much, which could lead you to the assumption that your assumption was the correct one, but even though one could infer that we were hiding, one could not in any way infer that we were hiding from the soldiers commissioned by our most beloved ruler, the fairy princess Ozma of Oz, for indeed—"

"If you're not hiding from Ozma's soldiers, who are you hiding from?" Zerie interrupted.

"Oh, from the most hideous of beasts, perhaps the most hideous of creatures that exist or ever did exist in the entirety of the world's time, although such things cannot be determined without a great deal more study and contemplation," Ednah said.

"Try to talk in shorter sentences," Vashti coached her. "You try it, Edmond."

"We're hiding from Kalidahs," Edmond said. Then he began to twist his hands together, turning to Ednah. "What if they can hear all this racket we're making? What if they're right above us now?"

"Kalidahs?" Zerie cut in. "Kalidahs don't live anywhere near here." She had heard of the fearsome creatures from Tabitha. Kalidah territory was in Munchkin Country, and they were now in Quadling Country.

"Kalidahs go wherever they please," the Glass Cat said. "It's one of the two things I have in common with them. We both wander the entire Land of Oz. And we both have razor-sharp claws."

Edmond cried out in fear and backed away from the cat.

"I thought Kalidahs were just a myth," Brink said. "Creatures with the heads of tigers and the bodies of bears. Or is it the other way around?"

"No, you're right, for a change," the Glass Cat said. "The tiger heads have sharp teeth and an intelligent feline brain. The bear bodies can walk upright and rend you with their fearsome claws." She daintily licked one glass paw as she spoke. "They're very vicious beasts. If they find us, they will surely kill you all."

.11.

"Are you positive that there are Kalidahs around here?" Vashti asked Ednah after an hour of hiding in the ditch.

"Two of the terrible things chased us off the road of yellow brick, and if we hadn't fallen into this ditch they certainly would have found us," Ednah began.

"Oh, what if we hadn't fallen?" Edmond said. "What if the Kalidahs had caught up to us before we fell through the bushes? If they'd caught us, they would have torn us apart for sure. And if they tore us apart—"

Ednah hugged him as he cried in fear. "They didn't catch us," she said simply.

"So what are we supposed to do?" Zerie asked Brink and Vashti. "We can't just hide here forever, but Kalidahs . . ." She wrapped her arms around herself, frightened. She'd never really thought much about the awful beasts—none had ever come near her village. But what would she do, face-to-face with a monster that wanted to attack her?

"I knew we might get caught by the Winged Monkeys, but I never realized there would be other dangerous things, too," Vashti said, echoing Zerie's thoughts. "We should've just stayed home."

"We didn't have that choice," Brink replied. "The Winged Monkeys were coming for us."

Zerie nodded, but Vashti sighed. "Then we should've let them take us. If we go back to the road right now, maybe the mounted soldiers will come back and we can turn ourselves in. At least we'd be safe from Kalidahs. I'd rather lose my talent than be killed by a wild beast."

Brink didn't answer, and Zerie wasn't sure what to say. She was terrified of the Kalidahs, too, but the idea of turning herself in made her furious.

"No," she finally said. "If we lose our talents, we lose ourselves. Vashti, if they captured you and put you in the Forbidden Fountain, the person who came back out wouldn't be you. She might look like you and talk like you and remember all the different weaving patterns that you know . . . but she wouldn't be the real you."

"Zerie's right," Brink said. "It isn't fair that Ozma should decide which parts of your personality you get to keep and which you don't. You've never used your magical talent to do anything wrong, so you shouldn't be punished."

"This is all very philosophical," the Glass Cat said, "but we are running out of nighttime. We won't reach Glinda's Palace by sitting in a ditch."

"Isn't there some other way we can go?" Zerie asked. "There's got to be a safer path."

"You are running from the leader of Oz, traveling through the wilderness to your only hope of help," the cat replied. "Nothing you're doing is safe. You won't be safe until you reach Glinda."

The words felt like a splash of cold water in her face. Zerie blinked a few times, trying to absorb what the cat was saying. She was right, of course. There was danger every way they turned, and no way out of it. Even going back home wouldn't be safe.

"But what do we do about the Kalidahs?" Vashti's voice sounded small.

"Hide from them!" cried Edmond. "What if they catch you? What if they eat you?"

"No more what-ifs," Zerie cut him off. "We can't hide forever."

"We also can't just climb out of here and start walking," Brink said. "I'll go look around and see if there are any signs of them." Without waiting for an answer, he tickled some of the red branches out of the way and clambered from the ditch.

"That was brave," Zerie said to Vashti. "Brink has really been great. I always thought he was kind of annoying before, but I was wrong."

"Me too," Vashti replied. "I paid so much attention to Ned that I never even noticed Brink. But without him I'm not sure we would've made it this far." She stood up to peer through the branches after him. "Plus, he's cute. I never noticed that either."

Cute? Zerie thought, surprised. *Brink?*

She'd never considered how he looked. Ned was the handsome one, with his broad shoulders and his muscled arms. And his friendly smile. And his big brown eyes.

But Brink? The whole idea of Brink being cute just seemed . . . strange.

Zerie had liked Ned forever. And she had always thought of Brink as just being Ned's annoying little brother. She'd never even really thought of him as a *boy*.

"What if the Kalidahs find him and he never comes back?" Edmond moaned. "What if he never comes back and we never know what happened to him? What if we hear them fighting, and then he comes back here and he's hurt? And what if he comes back and leads the Kalidahs right to us? What if they trap us in this ditch and we can't escape them?"

Zerie tried to tune him out. There was no point in trying to coach Edmond to drop his worrying right now. It was clear that both the Flutterbudget and the Rigmarole couldn't control themselves as well when they were scared or upset.

Just as Ednah was about to start whatever long-winded answer she was planning, Brink stuck his head back through the bushes. "I don't see anything or hear anything or smell anything," he said. "Let's go."

"Don't we need a plan?" Vashti asked anxiously. "Are we going back to the road?"

"No," said the Glass Cat. "I told you there would be soldiers, and there were."

"I hate to say it, but I agree with her," Zerie said. "We barely made it a mile before we heard the horses. The soldiers must be patrolling the road."

"Then how do we get there? Just wander around and hope we don't get eaten by a Kalidah?" Vashti demanded.

"We don't wander. We head south," the cat replied. "It will be difficult. There are The Trenches, and then the Tilted Forest, before we reach Glinda's Palace."

"What do you mean, trenches?" Brink asked, swinging back down into the ditch.

He held onto one of the overhead branches for a moment before he jumped, and Zerie noticed that his arms were nearly as muscular as Ned's. How had she never seen that?

"The Trenches are trenches, obviously," said the Glass Cat. "This ditch is probably one of the outlying trenches. Most of them are far deeper and far wider."

"Trenches?" Zerie said. Her heart sank at the thought of having to climb in and out of holes in the dark. "Can we make our way around them somehow?"

"Perhaps. But it would require you to walk at least

twenty miles in each direction every time," the cat replied. "Shall we go?"

"I guess." Zerie reluctantly turned toward Ednah and Edmond. "Do you two . . . want to come with us?"

"Good heavens, no!" cried Edmond. "You could be caught by soldiers! You could be caught by Kalidahs! And what if you get into a trench that you can't get out of? What if you're climbing out of a trench and your rope breaks and you fall? What if there's a Kalidah at the bottom when you fall? What if it's a hungry Kalidah and you—"

"We thank you for the offer," Ednah put in, "though whether it be generous or self-serving is entirely unclear, largely due to the fact that our acquaintance has been one of only an hour or possibly a little more than an hour, or possibly a few minutes less than an hour. Without a reliable clock it is nearly impossible to know for certain how many minutes have ticked by, and a reliable clock—"

"Okay, well, good luck!" Brink interrupted.

Vashti laid her hand on Ednah's arm. "Remember to use fewer words. And Edmond, stop saying 'what if.' If you learn to calm down a bit, you two can live anywhere in Oz, because you won't be a Rigmarole and a Flutterbudget anymore."

Edmond and Ednah watched with worried eyes as the three friends climbed up out of the ditch. They had to tickle their way through the bushes, and Zerie was glad when Brink got to the top and reached back to help her. He pulled her up onto the ground and smiled.

Zerie jerked her hand away from his, her cheeks heating up. Why was she suddenly so aware of Brink's hands, and his arms, and his smile?

Vashti's right, he is cute, she thought. *And now I can't stop thinking about it.*

"It's almost midnight. We'd better start walking if we want to get anywhere tonight," the Glass Cat said, winding her way between their legs.

"How can we tell if a Kalidah is nearby?" Zerie asked in a low voice.

"Usually the snarling and growling gives them away," the cat replied, calmly picking her way through a patch of tickle bushes.

"We'll stick together and keep our ears open," Brink said, helping Vashti from the ditch. He linked his arm through hers and held his other arm out to Zerie.

She was almost afraid to touch him, but it would look weird not to.

"Tigers with bear bodies," she murmured, sliding her arm through Brink's and trying hard to ignore the little tingle she felt as her skin touched his. "That's what we're looking for. Tigers and bears."

"Tigers and bears," Vashti repeated, her voice shrill with fear.

"Tigers and bears," Brink agreed.

Arm in arm, they began to walk. Zerie felt better holding on to her friends, as if she were not one girl, but part of a bigger thing.

Friends are always strongest together. If any of those tiger-bears tried to attack, it would be facing all three of them, not just one.

They moved faster and faster until they were practically skipping, following the Glass Cat through the wilderness.

Even though she was terrified, Zerie felt strangely free. She had her friends, and she had her talent, and she was traveling the Land of Oz— just like she'd always wanted to for her whole life. If that meant she had to be scared sometimes, she could handle it.

The first trench appeared about three miles away.

"The Trenches? This is a cliff!" Vashti cried when the ground suddenly dropped away before their feet.

"How many of these are there?" Zerie asked, gazing down into the dark chasm. She couldn't see the bottom.

"Four or five," the cat said. "Or six. I forget."

"Well, what are they?" Vashti demanded. "When you said trenches I thought you just meant holes in the ground."

"Technically, that's what a trench is." The Glass Cat stretched her back as she spoke. "These Trenches are exceptionally large, cutting through many miles of the wilderness. Oh, and there are quite a few different ecosystems in them, as well. Nothing very interesting, of course." She jumped off the edge, her glass body glittering in the starlight until she fell out of sight.

"I'm not doing that," Brink said. "Cats might land on their feet, but I don't."

"What did she mean, different ecosystems?" Vashti asked.

Brink shrugged. "Did Tabitha have any stories about The Trenches?"

"Nope," Zerie said. "I've never even heard of them before."

"I wish I'd still never heard of them!" Vashti said, peering over the edge of the cliff. "How deep do you think it is?"

"Deep," Brink replied. "If we can't see the bottom, we have to assume it's at least twenty or thirty feet."

"Maybe we can find something to use as a bridge," Zerie suggested. "Like a tall tree we could cut down and put across. Then we could walk over it."

"There are no tall trees around here, just the tickle bushes," Vashti said. "And we don't have an axe, anyway."

"Well, there are trees on the other side. It looks like a jungle over there. Maybe the whole landscape is different on that side of the trench." Zerie squinted, trying to see across, but the most she could make out were the shapes of shaggy trees and vines. "Maybe that's what the cat meant by a different ecosystem."

"The cat's already across!" Brink pointed to the other side of the trench. Tthe Glass Cat was climbing up the wall. "It must be pretty narrow at the bottom if she jumped in and ran across so fast."

"It's hard to tell in the dark." Zerie squinted across the trench. "I guess it's deeper than it is wide. I'd say it's probably only fifteen feet or so wide."

"That's still too far to jump. I wish we could climb like the cat," Vashti said. "Or that we had a rope."

"A rope!" Zerie cried. "Maybe I can make one." She stared across the trench, focusing on the closest tree she could see. A vine looped down from its branches and twined itself around the trunk. Zerie closed her eyes and pictured the vine growing . . . growing . . . longer and longer until it could reach over the trench.

"What are you doing?" Brink's voice brought her out of her imagining.

Zerie opened her eyes and tried to see the vine again. It was hanging just as it had been before. "I was trying to use my magic to make that vine grow longer so we could use it as a rope," she said. "But it didn't work at all."

"That's a bow-vine. They never get any longer than that," Vashti said. "Us weavers use them all the time because once they attach to something, they tie themselves into a bow and stay put. You have to untie them from the tree to harvest them, which is a pain because they never want to be untied. But they make really strong baskets, since they always stay tied."

"Would they make good ropes?" Brink asked.

"Sure, if you tie a few together, they would stay tied

forever," Vashti replied. "But they're kind of short. The longest one I ever saw was about eight feet."

"So I can't make it longer because that would be unnatural," Zerie said. "I guess I thought that speeding up the growth would help, but I can't make it do what nature doesn't want it to."

"It was a good idea, though," Brink said.

"Maybe . . ." Vashti said hesitantly. "Maybe I could levitate us all across."

"That's a great idea! Try it," Zerie told her.

"Okay." Vashti shook out her arms and shoulders to relax herself. Then she took hold of Zerie and Brink's hands, and puckered her brow in concentration.

Nothing happened. Zerie shot Brink a questioning look, and he shook his head. He didn't feel anything either. Vashti closed her eyes and kept trying.

A moment later, she said excitedly, "It's working!"

Zerie frowned. Her feet were still on the ground. So were Brink's. But Vashti was rising into the air, floating six inches above the grass. She wore an eager smile.

Brink slipped his hand out of Vashti's and motioned for Zerie to do the same. She did, trying to let go softly so that Vashti wouldn't notice. It seemed to work, because Vashti rose higher into the air without opening her eyes.

"Picture us floating over the trench," Zerie told her, hoping her friend would still think they were all together. She didn't want Vashti to realize that anything had gone wrong—she was already feeling insecure about her talent.

Vashti rose farther off the ground, but she stayed right above them.

Brink pulled Zerie close so he could whisper in her ear. "Speed her up," he murmured. "Like you did back in the woods at home. She could lift things, but you had to move them."

He reached out and—as gently as possible—pushed Vashti's legs, aiming her toward the trench. Immediately, Zerie screwed her eyes shut and pictured Vashti moving across the trench, landing on the far side where the Glass Cat was now waiting.

"Wha—" Vashti's cry of surprise turned to a scream, and Zerie's eyes snapped open. Vashti had felt Brink pushing her, and it had broken her concentration. Her levitation faltered, and she began to sink.

But she was already over the open trench, moving fast with Zerie's magic.

"Vashti, no! Pull yourself back up!" Brink cried. "Concentrate!"

Vashti kept sinking. Zerie couldn't force herself to look away, or to close her eyes and use her talent. Her best friend was suspended over a deep pit, and she was going to fall!

Vashti's panicked eyes met hers, and Zerie instantly felt a surge of magic. She wouldn't let Vashti plummet. Would not.

"Levitate!" she yelled at her best friend. "You can do it! You are doing it!"

This time Zerie didn't need to close her eyes or to spend any time picturing what would happen. She thought about Vashti moving fast, fast, fast . . . and Vashti did. She flew like a slingshot over the trench and crashed to the ground on the far side. She was safe.

Zerie felt weak with relief when she saw Vashti stand up. But even from this distance, she could see how upset her friend's expression was.

"You did it, Vashti!" Brink called. "You levitated yourself for the whole time."

"I almost fell, and I bet I never even got you two off the ground," Vashti called back. "Did I?"

Zerie still felt too exhausted to talk, so she was glad when Brink kept going. "You only started to fall because I distracted you—I'm sorry," he called. "I gave you a push so Zerie could keep you moving quickly."

"It was teamwork, just like what we did that time with Tabitha," Zerie called weakly. "Friends are strongest together, remember? It worked great, Vash."

Vashti still looked as if she might cry, and Zerie felt helpless to comfort her.

"Two down, two to go!" Brink called cheerfully. "Vashti, since the bow-vines are on your side, maybe you can weave a bunch of them together to make a rope."

"Sure. Yeah, I can do that." Vashti snapped out of her funk and turned to the trees to gather some vines.

Brink sat down next to Zerie. "You're really good at that—making people feel better," she told him.

"Vashti gets upset about her talent not working the way she wants. I figured it would be helpful to have her work on something she's fantastic at, like weaving. She's going to make us the strongest rope ever," Brink said. "And then she'll feel more confident again."

"See? You're really good at it. I think cheering people up is your other magical talent," Zerie told him.

He blushed. It made Zerie feel embarrassed suddenly, and her face heated up, too.

"Are you okay?" Brink asked after a moment. "You usually need to concentrate and visualize before you move something fast, but this time you just . . . you just did it."

She nodded. "I'm all right—tired, but all right."

"You've been getting stronger and stronger on this trip," he said. "I guess I'd better start practicing my magic if I want to keep up with you."

"Oh, please. You'll never keep up with me," she said, teasing.

Brink laughed and shoved her arm.

"Make an illusion now, while we're waiting," she suggested.

"Okay." Brink sat still for a long time, so long that Zerie wondered if he was falling asleep. Then suddenly she noticed something out of the corner of her eye—somebody approached them and sank down onto the ground next to her.

Zerie turned, and jumped in surprise. The person on the grass was her. It was Zerie Greenapple in her gingham shirt and blue linen pants, with her curly red hair and her green eyes, wearing a slight smile.

"Aaahhh! Make that stop!" Zerie cried.

The other Zerie vanished.

"Why? What's wrong?" Brink asked.

"That was me!" Zerie said. "That was weird. I mean, it was me."

"Right. I told you I can only do things that I see all the time, that I know really well," Brink said. "I've seen you constantly today." He was looking at her with such intensity that Zerie felt exposed all of a sudden, as if he could tell what she was thinking and feeling. It made her feel squirmy, and she got to her feet and moved away from him.

"Vash! Is the rope almost done?" she called.

"Yes. But I'm not sure I can throw it all the way over," Vashti replied from the other side of the trench. "What if it falls into the trench?"

"Oh, for heaven's sake," the Glass Cat put in, stretching her back into a high arch. "You incompetent people will spend the whole night trying to get through one trench! I will take the rope over to them."

She grabbed one end of the bow-vine rope in her glass teeth and leapt to the bottom of the trench. In another minute, Zerie could see her climbing up the wall on their side, the rope trailing behind her.

"It must be nice to be a cat," Brink commented.

"Especially one made of glass—she's indestructible," Zerie agreed.

The cat clawed her way up over the edge of the chasm and dropped the vine from her mouth with a puckered expression. "That tastes terrible," she spat. "Sometimes I wonder why I put myself through these things." And with that, she jumped back into the trench.

Zerie and Brink laughed.

"How should we do this?" Zerie asked. "If we tie the rope to one of the tickle bushes, we can both climb down it. But then we won't be able to untie it and use it to climb back up the other side."

"I'm making another one," Vashti called. "It will take too long if we have to keep passing the rope back and forth. By the time you get to the bottom, I'll be able to lower this new rope down to you."

"Good idea!" Zerie replied. "We'd be lost without you."

Brink tied the vine rope around the thickest tickle bush he could find. Then Zerie slung her bag over her shoulder, took a deep breath, and climbed over the edge of the trench. She'd always been a good climber—growing up in an orchard meant she could climb trees before she could walk. She lowered herself quickly to the bottom, about twenty-five feet down. But Brink took a little longer. He clung tightly to the rope and moved slowly.

I guess Brink isn't used to climbing, Zerie thought, watching him as he moved. She couldn't help herself—she just wanted to stare at him.

He really was cute, maybe even more than Ned. Ned was handsome, but he didn't have the same entertaining personality that Brink did. Brink liked to tease her, and that was fun. And Brink was incredibly helpful whenever she needed him. It wasn't something she would have noticed back home, but out in the wilderness she was learning just how dependable and kind he really was.

"This place is crazy." Brink was panting when he finally reached the bottom.

"Oh. Yeah, I guess it is," Zerie replied.

The truth was, she'd been so preoccupied by thinking about Brink that she hadn't even looked around yet. Now that she did, she saw that he was right.

The trench wasn't very wide, but there were two entirely different environments in it. The side they had just come from was covered with the reddish tickle bushes. They grew sideways on the wall and all along the floor. Nothing but tickle bushes as far as the eye could see, running along that one side and right up to the middle of the trench. But the other side was covered in deep purple chewing-gum trees—they didn't reach the top of the trench, which is why she hadn't noticed them from above. Still, they grew so thickly that it was like a small jungle at the bottom of the trench, filled with trees and vines . . . all of them growing right up to the same straight line in the middle. It looked as if a giant had drawn a line dividing the trench length-wise, and then colored one side red and the other side purple.

"Weird." Brink held out his hand. "Let's go."

"Okay." Zerie put her hand in his, trying to be casual about it. They were just two friends helping each other through a trench. It wasn't as if they were holding hands.

Together they stepped over the line that divided the bushes from the jungle. Brink shoved aside purple branches and vines with his free hand, and within two minutes they reached the far wall.

"Vashti! Can you see us?" Zerie called.

"Not really, it's pretty dark down there," Vashti's voice came back. "But I'll drop the rope down near your voice."

Another bow-vine rope crashed through the treetops. Brink jumped up to unsnag it from a gum-tree branch, and then he tied it around Zerie's waist. "Ready?" he yelled to Vashti.

"I have it tied to a tree up here," she called back.

Zerie took hold of the rope and climbed quickly to the top. Vashti helped her over the edge and hugged her. Then they untied the rope from Zerie's waist and dropped that end back down for Brink.

Vashti handed Zerie a purple flower from one of the trees. "It's good," she said.

Zerie gingerly put the flower in her mouth, where it instantly melted into a chewy, fruity blob of gum.

By the time Brink made it to the top, both girls had learned how to blow big purple bubbles, and the eastern sky was turning gray. It had been a long night.

"How far to the next trench?" Brink asked the Glass Cat. "Can we make it tonight?"

"About a mile through the jungle," she replied. "Then we'll come to the trench that is half jungle, half desert."

"Desert?" Zerie said. "Are they all like this, split into two different environments?"

"Of course," said the cat, as if it were the most obvious thing in the world. "I told you there would be different ecosystems. It's The Trenches."

"So each one has two different things? What comes after the desert?" Brink asked.

The cat's tail flicked angrily. "How should I know? I'm intelligent enough not to venture across a desert. I've always stopped at that trench before."

"Well, I think we should wait until tomorrow night to try the desert one," Vashti said. "If we cross the next trench tonight, we'll end up on the desert side when the sun comes up. That wouldn't be good."

A sudden growl caught their attention.

Zerie gazed across the trench they just came from—and her heart stopped. There on the other side stood the most fearsome creature she'd ever seen.

The wide green eyes of a tiger met hers, and the tiger's lips drew back in a snarl, revealing long, sharp teeth.

With another growl, the thing stood on two hind legs, its dark form rising up like a nightmare to six-foot height. It was a bear—its entire body was covered in dark, thick fur, except for the claws, which gleamed white.

"A Kalidah!" Vashti screamed.

Zerie couldn't speak at all, she was so frightened.

"No, it's two Kalidahs," the Glass Cat said casually.

Sure enough, another nightmare creature appeared behind the first, roaring at them over the trench.

"Can those things climb?" Brink asked.

"Not as well as a regular tiger," the cat replied. "But you've left a rope hanging there to help them."

As she spoke, the first Kalidah grabbed on to the vine rope with its bear hands and swung down into the trench.

"They're coming after us," Zerie cried. "Run!"

.12.

Zerie was halfway through the jungle when she realized her friends weren't with her. She skidded to a stop and shook her head. She must've used her magic and run too fast, leaving them behind. She hadn't even been aware that she was doing it, but the fear of the Kalidahs had driven her.

She closed her eyes and pictured the edge of the trench where she'd left Brink and Vashti, and she imagined the path back there.

When she opened her eyes, her friends were staring at her.

"Did you just go somewhere?" Brink asked.

"Yes, I ran, and I guess it was fast because you two couldn't catch up," she replied.

"Catch up? You were only gone for a minute," Vashti said. "We didn't even start."

"Well, start," Zerie said. "Those Kalidahs are coming. We have to run!"

"Run where?" Vashti asked frantically. "The cat said it's a desert after the next trench. There's nowhere to hide! They'll catch us for sure."

"Okay. Okay, okay, okay," Zerie murmured, trying to think. "So we have to hide. They never found us in the ditch with Ednah and Edmond. Maybe they couldn't get through the tickle bushes."

"Tickle bushes! I think I can do that illusion," Brink said. "I'll make it look like the bushes are growing over the top of the trench. Both the Kalidahs are down inside it now." He stared at the trench, concentrating.

"I can help." Zerie took his hand, closed her eyes, and pictured the bushes on the far side of the hole. They could grow very thick, their branches long and intertwining. She imagined the bushes growing, maturing, tangling together, extending out over the chasm until they reached the tops of the trees that grew inside the trench.

"You're doing it!" Vashti whispered.

Zerie opened her eyes. The trench had a cover now, red tickle bushes lying like a carpet over the top. "How much of that is illusion and how much is real?" she asked.

"It doesn't matter. You made them grow and then I used the new, bigger bushes as the basis for my illusion," Brink said. "I didn't know I could do that."

"I still hear the Kalidahs," Vashti said. "If they figure it out, they'll be up here in no time. Where should we go?"

"To the next trench," the Glass Cat said. "Where else?" She took off running into the jungle. The three friends followed.

Zerie felt as if she was jogging through molasses. She'd run farther than this before in no time at all. Her whole body yearned to move faster, as fast as her magical talent could take her. She'd made Brink and Vashti move as fast as she did once, when the Foot Hills were about to stomp them. But making the tickle bushes grow had used a lot of magic, and she felt tired. She wasn't sure how much strength she had left. So for now she just ran along slowly, following the cat.

"Where's the trench?" Brink asked breathlessly

when they'd been running for ten minutes. "The cat said it was a mile in, so maybe we should slow down. If it just drops off in the middle of this jungle, we could fall in before we ever even see it coming."

Vashti stopped running immediately, panting. Zerie stopped, too, though she wasn't even winded.

"Do you hear anything?" Zerie asked. "Maybe those Kalidahs are still down in the last trench. Maybe the illusion worked and they think they're trapped."

"I doubt it. I don't think the illusion would last after I stopped paying attention to it, do you?" Brink asked. "The only bushes over that trench now are the ones you grew there."

"Where's the Glass Cat?" Vashti peered through the jungle, which was getting lighter every minute. The sun was rising above the canopy of purple gum trees.

"She was there a minute ago," Zerie said, pushing aside some of the vines to get a better view. All she saw were trees and vines. No cat.

"Well, we know which way to go. She'll turn up."

Brink began walking again, so Zerie and Vashti did, too, though Zerie couldn't shake the feeling of unease about the cat. She didn't like being in a jungle without their guide.

"There." Brink pointed. "I think that must be the trench. It's so bright."

Zerie nodded. Up ahead, a light shone through the dense trees. The three friends crept along slowly, eyes on the ground, waiting to see a drop-off.

"Look up," Vashti said, grabbing Zerie's arm. "It's the desert on the other side."

Sure enough, when Zerie gazed straight ahead, she saw pale sand, blazing in the first beams of dawn. She looked down, searching for the edge of this trench. They had to be standing right on top of it.

"Here. It's hard to make out." Brink knelt and ran his hand along the plants on the ground. "The chasm starts right here, but the underbrush and the trees grow right over the edge so you can't see it."

"That's scary," Zerie said. She took hold of the closest tree trunk and leaned out over the side of the trench. Far below, she could see a line along the bottom, dividing the trench in half. This side of the trench was jungle. The other side was desert. It looked as if there was a boundary on the ground, and the plants and the sand each stayed on their own side. The line ran as far as the horizon in both directions. "How will we get down this time?"

"I brought the last rope with us," Vashti said. "But I don't want to leave it hanging again for the Kalidahs. Can we climb down this one by ourselves? There are vines and trees growing from the wall."

Suddenly a snarl echoed through the air, followed by the sound of something crashing through the trees.

"What do we do?" Zerie asked, trying not to panic.

"Vashti, you can levitate yourself down into the trench," Brink said. "Zerie, climb down and start making the jungle plants grow. We'll have to stick to the jungle side for now. We have to build a hiding place at the bottom—one where we can spend the day and the Kalidahs won't find us."

"But what about you?" Zerie cried.

"I'm going to use my talent," he answered. "Wish me luck."

The growling and snarling grew closer.

"Float," Vashti whispered, closing her eyes. "Float."

She lifted off the ground, and Zerie gave her a gentle nudge toward the trench. "Don't go over it, go into it," she reminded her friend.

Vashti didn't answer, but she began to float down into the chasm.

The trees nearby were shaking, leaves and vines

flying as the Kalidahs smashed their way through the jungle.

Zerie grabbed a vine and lowered herself over the edge so the Kalidahs wouldn't be able to see her. There she stopped, pressed up against the wall, clinging to the plants. She couldn't leave Brink.

Peering over the edge, she saw him kneeling, motionless. And then there he was again, in the trees, away from the trench, walking east. And again, another Brink, walking west.

Zerie stared, awestruck, as she appeared next to him, and again. Two Zeries, going in different directions. Then Vashti appeared in both places. Zerie was stunned by how perfect Brink's illusion was—the fake Zerie and Vashti and Brink looked exactly like the real ones. The illusory friends began to run, one set of three going east and the other going west.

Please let it work, Zerie thought. *Please.*

There was a confused bellowing from the Kalidahs. And then one dark form headed off to the right, crashing through the trees after the first fake friends. The other went left, following the second illusion, snarling and rending the jungle.

Zerie sighed in relief. The Kalidahs were off their

trail—for now, at least. She pulled herself back up over the edge and hurried over to Brink. He still sat silently, not even seeming to notice her. "I know you're holding the illusion for as long as you can," she told him. "You keep concentrating, and then when the Kalidahs are far away, we'll both climb down together."

He didn't say anything, but his hand reached out and took hers.

The sounds of the Kalidahs trailed off in different directions, and finally there was silence.

"I can't tell if the illusions are still there. It's too far away," Brink said.

"Then we'd better get down into the trench," Zerie replied. "The sun is up now, so we have to hurry before anything can see us. I'll build a shelter from jungle plants and we'll be safe."

"You're right, we'd better go before they come back," Brink agreed. "But remember what the Glass Cat said—we'll never be safe."

.13.

Vashti was waiting for them at the bottom of the trench. This one was wider than the last, so Zerie couldn't see the boundary line where the jungle met the desert until they'd walked south for a few minutes.

"I thought we could set up camp near the line," Vashti said. "You can grow all the trees and vines into a sort of fort, Zerie, and then tonight we can sneak out right over the line and get up the far side as soon as possible."

"How are we going to get up it?" Brink asked as Zerie began to age the trees and vines.

She concentrated on making the trees as big as

possible, knowing the bow-vines wouldn't get much longer. But if she took the young vines and aged them to their full length, Vashti would be able to weave them together into a roof.

"I don't know," Vashti answered. "I still have the vine rope, and I can make more. But that doesn't help us unless somebody can climb up the wall on the desert side."

"It's all just sand and dirt, though. How can we climb with no plants to hang on to?" Brink said. "That wall has to be fifty feet high!"

"I'm hoping the Glass Cat shows up. I can't think of any other way to get out of this trench," Vashti replied. "She can climb anything! She's a cat!"

"These trees are as tall as they're going to get," Zerie announced, her voice tired. "I aged all the vines I could see so they're as long as they can be."

"Okay. I'll take the first watch since you two are tired from using your talents," Vashti said, not looking Zerie in the eye. "I'll weave the bow-vines together to make more of a shelter so the Kalidahs can't see us from above."

She reached for the nearest vine, tugging to free it from the tree it was wrapped around. "Ugh. I hate when bow-vines get knotted," she said. "It won't come loose."

"I'll help." Brink grabbed the vine and pulled along with Vashti. This time the vine came slithering down from the trunk—and with it came a Kalidah.

Vashti screamed.

The beast roared, baring its teeth, and now that it was light out, Zerie could see that there were two rows of teeth in the tigerlike mouth. The Kalidah landed on the ground on all fours and snarled at them, advancing toward them very slowly.

"What do we do? What do we do?" Vashti cried.

"Find a weapon," Zerie said. "Anything you can use!"

"Sticks!" Brink grabbed a branch and yanked on it until it snapped off the gum tree.

The Kalidah stood on its hind legs, rising up to its full bear height. It was taller than any of them, and Zerie felt rooted to the ground in terror.

Run, a voice in her mind told her. *Use your talent and run fast.*

Zerie grabbed Brink's hand to take him with her. But she couldn't get to Vashti because the Kalidah was in between them. The fear made Zerie's brain feel sluggish. She was so scared, she wasn't even sure her magic would work.

"How would we get up the wall, anyway?" Brink said, as if he knew what Zerie was thinking.

"Make another illusion," she told him.

"I can't. I'm trying, but it won't work." Brink shoved the tree branch into her hands and grabbed for another one.

The Kalidah growled again and swiped at Vashti, its razor-sharp claws coming within an inch of her face. Vashti jerked backward and stumbled against a tree trunk. "Help me! Zerie, do something!"

"Hey! Hey, nasty Kalidah! Come this way!" Zerie yelled. She waved her arms and jumped around, trying to get the monster's attention. When its eyes fixed on her, though, she had no idea what to do. The Kalidah turned and advanced on her and Brink, its teeth dripping saliva and a low growl in its throat.

Zerie gripped the tree branch tightly and swung it like a club, whacking the beast in the side. It roared, grabbed the branch with its paw, and tore it out of Zerie's hands.

The momentum threw Zerie to the ground and she lay there, stunned. She'd never felt anything so strong before. One swipe of the Kalidah's massive arm could kill her.

"Run, Zerie, move fast," Brink said from somewhere above her. Zerie couldn't focus. She thought about moving, but nothing happened.

The Kalidah roared, raising its arm. Zerie rolled onto her back and watched as the claws came rushing down at her.

"No!" Brink threw himself on top of Zerie, swinging another tree branch at the beast.

The Kalidah knocked this branch away, too, and lunged at them in fury. Zerie screwed her eyes shut and waited for the blow. It didn't come.

"Zerie, help." Vashti's voice sounded thin and frightened.

Zerie opened her eyes—and gasped.

The Kalidah was levitating. It floated in the air over their heads, snarling and clawing at the treetops.

"Vash, your talent . . ." Zerie breathed. She shot a look at her friend. Vashti held her arms straight, out in front of her, staring at the Kalidah in the air, shaking from the effort of levitating the huge creature.

"I can't hold it for long. I don't know what to do," Vashti said through clenched teeth.

"The branch," Brink said. "Look, it's sharp where I broke it from the tree." He snatched up the thick piece of wood and held it upright underneath the Kalidah. The end was jagged and scary looking. "If you drop the Kalidah, it will fall on this."

"That will kill it," Vashti protested.

"Tabitha always said the only way to kill a Kalidah was to pierce its heart," Zerie said.

"But I don't want to kill it," Vashti said.

"What choice do we have? It's trying to kill us," Brink said.

"Oh, no," Vashti moaned. "I can't hold it up any-more. I don't want to kill anything."

"You're not," Zerie said. "We all are."

"There's got to be another way." Vashti was pale and sweating, and Zerie thought she might faint. "No . . ."

The Kalidah fell.

Zerie held tight to the branch, knowing she had to help Brink keep it upright. But as the creature plum-meted toward the makeshift spear, she turned her face away.

She couldn't bear to watch. Instead, Zerie felt the Kalidah's body hit the wood and heard the snarling suddenly stop. The Kalidah shuddered and then went still.

"It's dead," Brink said grimly.

The branch was heavy now, so she let go of it and the monster's body dropped to the ground.

"Oh, no," Vashti moaned. "Oh no, oh no, oh no . . ."

"We killed something," Zerie said quietly. "We're not supposed to kill things. Life is precious! Ozma outlawed killing years and years ago."

"Zerie—" Brink started.

"No! We killed something," she said, cutting him off. "This creature was alive a minute ago and now it's dead because of us. What have we turned into? Are we really this bad now?"

"Of course not," Brink said.

"It's not fair!" Zerie went on, anger rising in her chest. "We wouldn't even be out here getting attacked if Ozma would just let us use our talents! We weren't doing anything wrong with our magic back home. We're only doing bad things now because they chased us out of our homes and turned us into fugitives!"

"Zerie," he said again.

"It's not fair!" she yelled, filled with rage. "I'm not

a killer. I would never have done something like this before."

She turned to face the Kalidah, looking at its dead body for the first time. Its tiger eyes were still open, and Zerie couldn't take it. She didn't want to see its face like this. She wanted it to be gone.

"Age. Get old, old, old," she whispered, staring at the beast. "Fast. Age quickly. Age!"

Zerie felt the magic growing within her, filling her whole body. This wasn't what her talent was meant to be for, but she knew her anger would give her the power to use as much magic as she wanted.

The Kalidah began to wither, the disintegration of its body speeding up at her urging. First the fur became patchy, and then its body seemed to deflate.

"Faster!" Zerie yelled.

The rest of it went in a blur, the entire body decomposing in an instant until there was nothing left but a pile of dust that blew away into the sand on the other side of the line.

Zerie, spent, stared at the place where the Kalidah had been. Had she really done that? She felt like a little girl who'd just gotten over a temper tantrum—exhausted and embarrassed.

Brink was watching her, open-mouthed. Zerie turned away from him. She didn't want to talk about the magic she'd used.

"I want to go home," Vashti sobbed. "I hate this!"

Zerie scrambled over to her friend. She wrapped her arms around Vashti. "You saved me and Brink. You kept saying you couldn't use your talent and it wasn't a worthwhile talent . . . but it saved our lives, Vashti."

Vashti sniffled. "I don't need magic so much that I have to kill for it."

"You're not the one who killed the Kalidah," Zerie said. "You levitated it until you just couldn't do it anymore. I'm the one who put a spear underneath it."

"Oh, Zerie. What have we gotten ourselves into? We should have just done what our parents told us and not practiced magic." Vashti's voice sounded thick and her eyelids fluttered. Zerie could see that she was exhausted, both from climbing through The Trenches all night and from using her talent.

"We were just playing around in the woods with our best friends. We didn't know it would lead to all of this," Zerie said. "You need to sleep, Vash. I'll take the first watch."

Vashti nodded, already drifting off.

"You were amazing with your talent. I always knew you could be," Zerie told her.

Vashti smiled a little, and slept.

Zerie pulled her friend's jacket over her as a blanket, and then she stood up and went back over to where the Kalidah had been. Brink still sat where he'd been when they killed the beast. Zerie felt him watching her.

"You aged something until it turned to dust. Do you know how many years it takes for something to turn to dust?" Brink said.

"No, and I don't want to know." Zerie stared out over the boundary where the jungle ended and the desert began.

"That must've taken a huge amount of magic. Are you tired?" he asked.

"No. I'm mad." Zerie felt a tear on her cheek, and she swiped it away. "It's because of Princess Ozma and this stupid no-magic law that we're in this situation. I'm so angry at her."

"I wish I were as strong as you, Zerie," Brink said.

Zerie took a shuddering breath. "I don't feel strong. I feel terrible that we killed a living thing."

"So do I." Brink's tone was so sad that Zerie spun

around to look at him. He sat slumped on the ground, his face pale and his green eyes haunted. For the first time, it occurred to her that she hadn't been holding that tree branch alone. It had been Brink's idea in the first place.

"Oh, Brink," she breathed. "You feel guilty, too."

"Of course I do," he said. "I just couldn't have a magical tantrum about it like you did." He gave her a thin smile to show he was teasing.

"I'm sorry." Zerie went over and sat down next to Brink. "I was so busy thinking of my own feelings that I didn't even realize you'd feel the same way."

"I know you've always thought I was a pain in the neck, Zerie," he said. "But I never wanted to end up a killer any more than you did."

"A pain? We probably would've been caught already, or gotten killed ourselves, if you weren't with us," Zerie said. "Vashti and I need you."

"It's nice to hear you say that," Brink told her. "I feel like a tagalong with you and Vashti since you're such good friends."

"Well, you're my friend, too," Zerie said. "And I'm sorry I was being selfish about the Kalidah. I'm really upset about it . . . but I know you are, too." She leaned over to give him a hug, and Brink wrapped his arms around her.

Zerie sighed and snuggled into his embrace. His arms were warm, and she finally felt safe with her cheek against his broad chest.

Wait. What am I doing? she thought suddenly. She'd meant to give him a sympathetic hug, not to . . . well, not to hug him for real. Zerie stiffened in embarrassment. What must he think of her?

But Brink tightened his arms around her and rested his chin on her hair. If Zerie was hugging him for real, then he was hugging her back for real.

In spite of everything else, she smiled.

Maybe I never will be safe again, Zerie thought. *But this feels pretty close.*

.14.

The Glass Cat hadn't returned by the time the sun went down that evening. Luckily, the other Kalidah hadn't returned either, but Zerie and her friends knew that they couldn't stay there and wait.

"The desert side of the trench isn't so wide," Brink said, peering over the line from the jungle. The final rays of sun stretched over the sands and cast long shadows on the high desert wall of the trench. "I'd say half a mile. Maybe you can move us over there quickly, Zerie, so we won't be as easy to see."

Zerie shook her head. "I can't. I don't know how to describe it, but I just can't use my power right now. I feel as if it isn't even in me anymore, ever since . . ." Her words trailed off. She couldn't bring herself to say ". . . since I turned that Kalidah into dust."

Vashti bit her lip. " Out there on the sand, we'll be easy to spot if the other Kalidah is watching."

"Or any flying Ozma spies," Brink put in.

"Sorry," Zerie said quietly.

"It's not your fault, We're just trying to plan." Brink rubbed her arm to comfort her, sending little tingles up her spine.

"Can you do an illusion?" Vashti asked. "If you stared at the sand for a long time, could you make an illusion of sand to hide us while we walk?"

"I can try," Brink replied. "I'm not sure how I would make it move with us, though."

"I have the same problem with my talent. I can levitate, but I don't know how to move. Last night is the first time I've ever been able to move at all," Vashti said.

"You did a lot with your magic last night," Brink told her. "Would you be able to levitate us up to the top of the next wall?"

Vashti frowned. "I don't know. Last time I tried to levitate the three of us, I'm the only one who moved."

"But you've gotten stronger since then," Zerie pointed out. "Besides, what other choice do we have? We can't climb that wall."

Vashti still looked doubtful. Brink went over and stood next to her. "It will work either way, Vashti. You can levitate yourself to the top—you know that because that's how you got to the bottom. Even if you can't bring us all, you can go up and throw down the rope."

"That's true. I feel sure I can do that." Vashti brightened. "I didn't think so last night, but now that seems easy."

"Good. It's dark now. I think we should go." Brink stepped across the boundary and gazed at the sand. "I'll try to make a sand illusion to cover us."

"He's amazing, isn't he?" Vashti murmured. "He always makes me feel better."

"Me too," Zerie admitted.

"I guess it's just something about the Springer boys, huh?" Vashti said. She picked up her pack and headed off toward Brink.

Zerie felt as if she'd been stung by a bee—surprised, and not in a good way.

Something about the Springer boys. What did that

mean? Was Vashti saying that she now liked Brink, too? She had been talking about how nice and cute he was . . .

"Oh, no," Zerie whispered to herself. "We can't like the same boy again."

"Come on, Zerie," Brink called. "I think I've got the illusion going, but we all have to be together. I can only do a small one."

Zerie hurried over to join them, linking arms with Brink. Vashti took his other arm.

"Here we go," Brink said.

Zerie nodded. *Here we go again.*

They half-walked, half-skipped across the hot sand, wanting to move as quickly as they could. If Brink had an illusion over them, Zerie couldn't see it, and she felt completely exposed. She kept glancing up at the sky, expecting to see some kind of clockwork bird, or worse, an airship.

It didn't take long to reach the wall, and once they were there, Vashti had them all stand in a circle. "I'm going to do it," she said confidently. "I'm sick of being at the bottom of this awful trench. It's been nothing but bad luck for us. First the Glass Cat disappeared, and then the Kalidah attack . . ."

"Yes, let's get out of here," Zerie agreed. She didn't want to talk about the attack.

"Hold my hands," Vashti said. She stretched out her arms, and Brink took her hand. Then he reached for Zerie's hand, too.

"It'll be easier if we're all connected," he said. "More stable. Strongest together, remember?"

"Okay." Zerie reluctantly held his hand, trying to ignore how warm it felt, how nice it was to feel his fingers intertwine with hers. She grabbed Vashti's other hand, and they stood in a triangle.

Vashti looked up at the top of the trench and whispered, "Float."

Zerie felt as if a huge gust of wind was sweeping her off her feet, lifting her up. She gasped in surprise as they rose, all together, into the air. Zerie wished she could cheer on Vashti for doing it, but she didn't want to break her concentration. So instead she squeezed her friends' hands tighter and dared to look down.

They were twenty feet high already, floating straight up along the wall. Below them, the desert and the jungle stretched out together, the boundary between them straight as far as she could see. Zerie looked up. The moon was dark tonight, so she could see a million stars, and she felt as if she was floating right in the middle of them.

"It's amazing," Brink whispered.

She smiled at him. "It is."

The lip of the trench came up sooner than she was expecting. When Vashti set them all back on the ground, Zerie felt a surge of disappointment. "Vashti, that was incredible," she cried. "I felt like I was flying!"

Vashti grinned. "I can't believe I did it!"

"If you can do it again, that would be great," Brink said. "Look."

The girls both turned to where he was pointing. Zerie felt a wave of dizziness when she realized that the rocky ground they stood on was only about ten feet wide. The lip of the next trench was right in front of them.

"I thought they'd be getting wider, not narrower," Vashti said in surprise.

"The highland is narrower, but that trench is much wider than the last one," Brink replied. He took a few steps and inched up to the edge of the cliff. "And deeper," he added, peering over the side.

Zerie looked down into the trench. She could see the sandy desert bottom far below, because the sand was light enough to show up in the dark. It stretched out for a long time at the bottom of the trench and then stopped at a strange dark border. "What's on the other side? It's too dark to see," she said. "The Glass Cat didn't tell us what came after the jungle and the desert."

"We'll find out when we get there, I guess," Brink said. "Should we try to use the ropes to get down?"

"No, I'll levitate us down there," Vashti said. "I'm going to try to move us in the air, so we can land near the boundary instead of having to walk all the way across the desert."

"Aren't you too tired? You just used your talent on all three of us for the first time," Zerie said.

"It felt like nothing!" Vashti said happily. "I want to do more. If I can learn how to move us while we're in the air, I can just fly us right over the rest of The Trenches."

Zerie was doubtful, but Brink took Vashti's hand and grinned at her. "You're learning fast," he said.

Vashti smiled back, and Zerie felt a stab of worry. They were so sweet together, and Vashti was so happy. But Zerie liked Brink, too. It wasn't fair that they were stuck in this situation again, liking the same boy.

"Here we go," Vashti said, taking hold of Zerie. "Float to the border," she said. "To the border."

Zerie wondered if her friend was picturing the route in the air, the same way she would picture it on the ground if she were using her talent. She clung tightly to Vashti and Brink and enjoyed the strange floating sensation all the way down to the floor of the deep trench. When their feet touched the sand, they were only inches from the boundary line.

This time Vashti sat down as soon as they landed. "Okay, that made me tired," she said, lying back on the sand.

"But you did it. You moved us forward. Your talent is getting stronger so fast, just like Tabitha's did," Zerie said.

The second Tabitha's name left her lips, she felt a stab of worry. They'd been so scared for the past two days that she hadn't had much time to think about her friend.

But by now Tabitha must have been taken to Ozma. By now she might have been forced into the dreaded Water of Oblivion. Was Tabitha even Tabitha anymore? It was hard to imagine who she would be without her talent.

"You'd better rest for a while before we even try walking across to the other side, Vashti," Brink said, kneeling by the line where the desert ended. "Because this will be tough going. I'm not even sure we can walk here."

"Why?" Zerie knelt next to him.

"Don't you smell that?" Brink waved his hand in front of his nose. "It's a swamp."

"I guess it's a good thing the Glass Cat never came through this trench," Vashti said.

"Well, if she had, she could have warned us about it. This is bad." Zerie perched on the edge of the desert and examined the ground. This was the first time she'd looked at one of the boundaries up close. The edge of the desert was completely smooth and straight, like somebody had taken a huge saw and cut the ground in half. Right on the other side of the edge lay something soft and gooey. And smelly. It didn't look like solid ground. It looked like something else altogether.

"Ugh." Zerie gingerly stuck her finger into the dark muck and pulled it back covered in thick red mud. "It's like a giant mud puddle. I hope it's not deep."

"It's going to take forever to get through this,"

Brink said. "Even if the mud only comes up to our shins, it will be hard to walk in."

"I'll levitate us over it," Vashti said. "I just need to rest for a while."

Brink and Zerie exchanged worried glances. "Are you sure? You've been doing so much tonight," Brink said.

"I feel fine. Though I'm hungry." Vashti sat up and rummaged in her pack. "I'm almost out of food. All I have left are some hard peaches I picked back near the Foot Hills."

"We'll have to look for food when we get to the top," Zerie said. "Though it'll be a swamp up there, too. Maybe the next trench will have an orchard at the bottom." Just the idea of going through more trenches made her feel hopeless. It was hard to believe they'd been at the Foot Hills only two days before. She felt as if they'd been traveling in The Trenches forever.

"Can you make these riper?" Vashti asked, handing Zerie a hard peach. "I can hardly even bite into it. I picked them way before they were ready."

"Sure." Zerie stared at the peach in her hand and willed it to age, for its life cycle to speed up until it was ripe. Nothing happened. Frustrated, she closed her eyes and concentrated harder, picturing the fruit softening, expanding, becoming juicier.

Nothing.

Vashti and Brink didn't say anything as Zerie handed the peach back.

"My power is wiped out," Zerie said. "Or it's gone."

"It's because of what you did to the Kalidah," Brink told her. "To its body, I mean. You usually age a flower or a fruit, and that's no big deal. But to age something into nothingness, well, that's exhausting."

"I aged the Foot Hill into sand," Zerie said. "And I could still use my talent after that."

"But you were really tired after the Foot Hill. You slept all day," Brink reminded her. "And this must have used even more magic, because it was a living creature, not a rock."

"A dead living creature," Vashti said sadly.

Nobody said anything after that.

After a while, Vashti ate the hard peach, making a face with each bite. Then they all shared the last piece of bread in Brink's pack and had a tiny bit of water.

"I want to get to the top of the trench," Vashti said. "That swamp is horrible."

"Are you sure you aren't too tired?" Zerie asked,

worried. "I don't want you to drop us into the middle of it."

Vashti stuck her tongue out at Zerie. "Yes, I'm sure, Miss Worrywart."

She stood up, took their hands, and levitated them over the red ooze and up the steep cliff on the other side.

Zerie had stopped being worried by the time they reached the top. Maybe it was difficult for Vashti, but the whole experience of levitating made Zerie feel as light as a feather. It felt easy, like floating on the top of a lake in summertime, weightless. Somehow, when Vashti levitated them, it felt like flying.

Still, they had to walk for more than an hour through the swamp at the top, the thick mud pulling at their shoes with every step. There were annoying flies buzzing everywhere, and Zerie had to force herself to stop trying to decide if every single one was real or clockwork. She had a feeling that even the clockwork spies of Ozma wouldn't come near this foul-smelling place.

"It figures these two trenches would be the farthest apart," Brink complained as they trudged.

"I'm just glad the Glass Cat isn't here for this part.

Can you imagine how appalled she'd be?" Zerie replied.

"I hope she's okay. What do you think happened to her?" Vashti asked from behind them. Her voice sounded tired, and she moved slowly through the mud.

Brink doubled back and put his arm around Vashti to help her walk. "Thanks." Vashti smiled at him. "I'm okay, I just want to save my strength so I can get us over the next trench. How many more are there?"

"The cat didn't seem sure," Brink said. "And who knows where she is, anyway. If she even survived."

Zerie took Vashti's pack and slung it over her shoulder, but she wasn't sure if she should try to help Vashti walk—she and Brink might be having a romantic moment.

Zerie felt uncomfortable even thinking about that. Instead, she tried to keep their minds off the mud.

"I bet the Glass Cat is fine. She ran off once before, remember? She likes to roam."

"There's the edge. Let's hope this is the last one," Brink said.

The next trench was the weirdest one yet, shaped more like a shallow bowl than a split in the earth. But there was still a boundary line through the middle of it where the swamp ended and something else began—something dazzling in the darkness, gleaming white and silver with odd greenish patches. Zerie couldn't make out the wall on the other side of the trench.

"What is that? Snow?" Zerie asked.

"Whatever it is, it's got to be cleaner than this swamp. I'm taking us straight across this time," Vashti said.

"You're too tired," Brink protested.

"I'll sleep on the other side. Come on!" Vashti grabbed their hands, but it took a minute for her to be able to lift them all out of the thick red mud. Once they were free, they floated quickly across the bowl-like trench. Zerie marveled at how far her friend's talent had come in only one day.

Vashti set them down in the snow, except as soon as they touched it they knew it wasn't snow. It was ice.

"A glacier!" Brink cried, thrilled.

"I didn't know glaciers were that exciting," Zerie said. "It's just one more landscape where we can't find any food."

"But there's only one glacier in the Land of Oz, and

I've seen it before," Brink said. "This is the glacier that lies on the border of the Tilted Forest. It means we're done. We're finished with The Trenches!"

"Oh, thank goodness. I need to sleep," Vashti said. "How far is it to the woods?"

"I don't know, but I think we can make your bow-vine ropes into a sled and get there faster," he said. "From what I remember, the glacier sort of slopes down right into the Tilted Forest. Are you too tired to weave, Vashti?"

He took Vashti's pack and rummaged through it, pulling out the coiled ropes she'd made. "Tell me what to do, and I'll weave them," he suggested.

"No, I can weave in my sleep," Vashti said. "I just hope they hold up long enough." She set her pack on the ice, sat on top of it, and started unraveling the ropes and weaving the bow-vines into a sort of basket.

"You've been here before?" Zerie asked Brink. "Why didn't you say so?"

"I never knew about The Trenches. I just saw the glacier from the Tilted Forest," Brink replied. "My father took us there once when Ned and I were kids. It's a really crazy place. All the trees grow sideways."

"But . . . you didn't tell us you'd been there when

the Glass Cat mentioned it." Zerie wasn't sure why that fact bothered her, but it definitely did.

"It was a long time ago, and we took our horse and cart down the road of yellow brick to get to the forest," Brink said. "We weren't on the run from the Winged Monkeys, and we didn't have to cut through Foot Hills and The Trenches." He looked at her and frowned.

"So it's near the road?" Vashti asked, her fingers flying over the vines.

"I don't think there's anything south of the Tilted Forest except for Glinda's Palace," Brink replied. "We'll have no choice but to take the road once we make it through the woods."

Thinking about the road reminded Zerie of Ozma's spies—they'd almost caught up to her and her friends the last time they tried to follow the road. She glanced up at the sky, looking for birds or flying clockwork animals.

Then she looked down again and gasped. "Our feet are all muddy!"

"Well, yeah. We just slogged through a swamp," Brink said.

"No, I mean, we've left muddy prints all over the

ice and snow." Zerie frantically grabbed a handful of snow and began scrubbing her shoes with it.

"You're right, anything watching from above would see our prints." Brink joined in, cleaning off his shoes and doing Vashti's while she worked on the sled.

Zerie took several more handfuls of snow and spread them over any footprints she could see. "No more walking," she told her friends. "We have to climb into the sled as soon as it's finished. We can't risk leaving footprints."

Vashti yawned. "I'm so tired, but it can't be past midnight."

"Let's just get to the forest. Then you can sleep until morning," Brink said sympathetically. "We don't need to travel at night in the Tilted Forest."

"Why not?" Zerie asked.

"The trees grow at an angle there. It's almost like the whole woods is inside one gigantic trench. The trees grow sideways out from the walls, so if you're walking on the bottom, there's a whole layer of them crisscrossing above you. Nothing in the air will see us on the bottom of the forest." Brink took a vine from Vashti and began helping her weave, though he did it at a much slower pace.

Zerie grabbed another vine and pitched in, and soon they had a long, shallow basket that would fit the three of them sitting in a line.

"I'll go in front," Brink said. "Then Vashti in the middle and Zerie in back."

As they climbed into the sled, Zerie couldn't help thinking about the fact that he'd placed Vashti next to him, with her arms around his waist. But any thoughts like that flew out of her head as soon as they started sledding down the glacier. The ice was more slippery than any snow Zerie had ever played in, and the woven basket flew over it, bouncing up and down like mad.

Brink let out a whoop, and Zerie had to hang on to Vashti tightly to keep herself from shooting right out of the sled. The air whipped her curly hair into a frenzy, and Zerie thought for a moment that it was like using her talent, they were going so fast. She smiled and let herself enjoy it.

It was over too soon. The sled skidded to the bottom of the icy hill, dumping them all out onto a pile of frozen snow. The bow-vines were cut to shreds, but they had held up long enough.

Brink helped Vashti to her feet and led the way

inside the bizarre forest that lay at the foot of the glacier.

The trees were mostly pines and oaks, their trunks sticking straight out across the friends' path. "Will we have to climb over every single one of them?" Zerie asked.

"Yes, but not now. Vashti's ready to pass out." Brink climbed over one tree trunk and ducked underneath another one. "I think this is far enough into the woods. If we sleep here, we should be safe from airships seeing us."

Zerie looked up. Above her was tree after tree after tree, all of them growing sideways. It was like looking at the rungs of a ladder made by giants. She couldn't even see the sky.

Brink came over and stood next to her, following her gaze. "My father said there was an earthquake long, long ago, and that it split the land right down the middle. The whole forest fell into the hole and just kept growing. Some of the trees go left, and some go right, and some go up, and some go down. They used to point at the sky, but ever since they fell into the hole, they point at one another."

"And we're at the bottom of the hole. We couldn't

go through here at night. It's pitch black under all these trees," Zerie said.

"I told you daytime would be better," Brink whispered. "Besides, Vashti's already asleep. Do you want me to take first watch?"

"No, I will. You sleep," Zerie said.

Brink lay down next to Vashti and began snoring in about two minutes. Zerie sat on the closest tree trunk and watched them for a little while.

She really liked Brink. They hadn't talked about the other night, when she'd fallen asleep in his arms. It had felt wonderful at the time, but now she wasn't sure what to think. Because it was pretty obvious that Vashti liked Brink, too.

Zerie picked up an acorn and stared at it. She imagined it sprouting, growing, turning into a tall, strong oak. But nothing happened. Her talent didn't work at all.

Brink and Vashti say it's because I exhausted myself, Zerie thought. *But I know they're wrong.*

She remembered how it had felt to age the Kalidah's body. She'd been filled with rage—and sorrow, too, but it was mostly rage. She'd felt the anger coursing through her body, and she'd known it would give her magic strength. She'd known she could use it to do something extreme . . . and she'd also known that she shouldn't.

Grammy had always said magic came from feeling good. That using your talent made you happy, and the happiness gave you strength to use your talent. That's why magic was there to help people—because it was good.

But Zerie knew there had to be another side to it, as well. She'd never realized it back home, but after all she'd been through, she realized it now. If good feelings led to good magic, then bad feelings had to lead to bad magic. And her anger at Ozma had been a bad feeling. She'd felt all the negative energy, and she'd used it to blast that Kalidah into dust.

I shouldn't have done that, Zerie thought. *Using anger to fuel magic can only lead me to bad places, like the old Wicked Witches who caused so much trouble for Dorothy and the Wizard. Their magic came from their negative thoughts, and that's where my magical tantrum came from, too.*

Zerie sighed. She hated to admit it, but for the first time she understood why Ozma had outlawed magic.

She stood up and looked down at her two friends.

Zerie had a feeling that her talent was gone, that she'd erased all the good that used to drive it. And she didn't want to find out if using anger would make it work again. Aging that Kalidah had been satisfying for a moment, but she'd been miserable ever since.

She wondered, though: Maybe, just maybe, if she paid more attention to being good, her magic would come back.

She would start by letting her best friend have a crush on Brink. Zerie had let a boy come between them before, back when they both liked Ned. This time, she wasn't going to do that. Vashti was her friend, and Vashti liked Brink.

"So it's time for me to stay away from him," Zerie whispered. No matter how much she cared about Brink, she was going to keep ignoring her feelings for him.

No matter how hard that might be.

.15.

"Don't you think Princess Ozma knows that her Winged Monkeys can't see in the Tilted Forest?" Zerie asked after an hour of climbing through the trees the next day. "I wonder if she's sent more clockwork bird spies to watch this part of the country."

"Only if they know we're trying to get to Glinda," Brink said. "She can't possibly have spies watching the whole Land of Oz."

"The last time we saw soldiers was on the road of yellow brick, way back near the Foot Hills. And we don't even know if those soldiers spotted us," Vashti said. "They didn't follow us off the road or find us in the ditch with Ednah and Edmond."

"Right. So probably they lost track of us when we escaped from our village. As far as Ozma is concerned, we could be anywhere," Brink agreed.

Zerie bit her lip to keep her frustration from spilling out. Every time she spoke today, it seemed as if her friends were united against her. Vashti and Brink felt the same way about everything, and Zerie was the only one who disagreed.

"We don't know how many other spies might have seen us. There were about a gazillion flies in the swamp, and any one of them could have been a clockwork spy. We wouldn't know, and that fly could be reporting back to Ozma right this second." Zerie grabbed hold of an oak that grew sideways at about waist height and pulled herself up onto the trunk. She sat there for a moment, resting. Climbing over and under tree trunks was hard work.

"I guess so. But I'm still happy that we're traveling during the day. I'm sick of doing everything in the dark," Vashti said. "Even if it's a bigger risk, I like it."

"I didn't mean we shouldn't travel during the day, I was just saying that we can't assume it's safer here than it was anywhere else." Zerie tried to push away the feeling that they were mad at her. She wasn't trying to question Brink's suggestion that they switch to daytime travel. She was only trying to be sensible, but her friends seemed prickly about it.

"When I came here before, I was really young," Brink said after a few more minutes of walking. "I remembered the tree trunks being gigantic, but I always figured it was because I was so little then that the trees seemed huge. But you know what? They are huge."

Vashti laughed. "They are. Or is it just because we're used to seeing them go up and down instead of sideways? We don't usually have to climb through all the branches of a tree just to get past it."

"I like that part, though. When we came here before, Ned and I would hide in the branches like they were forts, and then we would play soldiers." Brink smiled. "How often do you get to play inside the top of a tree like that? Though I just liked to pretend it was a castle. Ned was the one who wanted to be a soldier in a fort."

They all walked in silence for a little while, climbing over the trees that grew near the ground, ducking under the ones that grew higher up on the steep walls, and shimmying through the ones whose tops crossed their path. Zerie thought about little Brink playing with his brother in these trees, never imagining that he'd grow up to travel through them as a fugitive.

"Do you think Ned is looking for you?" Zerie asked. "I'm sure my grammy is looking for me."

"I don't know," Brink said slowly. "My father would definitely want to find me. I'm not sure about Ned."

"I can't believe that," Vashti cried. "How could he not want to find you?"

Brink shrugged.

"My brothers and sisters probably want to know what happened to me, but I don't know if most of them would ever leave the village to search," Zerie said. "They've all got their responsibilities in the orchard, and Zelzah has her baby. Zepho would look for me, though. He's like me—and he always wanted to see what was down the road."

"My parents have probably been up and down the road five times by now," Vashti said. "You don't suppose Ozma's soldiers took them, do you? Just because they're related to us and we were practicing magic?"

The thought was so awful that Zerie had to stop walking and sit for a moment. The Tilted Forest was beautiful, from the pink-tinged leaves of the trees to the deep red ivy that covered the forest floor. Here and there, small heart-shaped red flowers sprang up in patches among the underbrush. At any other time, Zerie would have found this place magical. Now, all she could think about was the danger she and her family were in.

"I don't believe Ozma would do that," Brink said. "Just because people are in the same family doesn't mean they behave the same way, or think the same things, or even tell each other what they're doing. Ozma wouldn't assume that the whole family was guilty just because one person was using magic."

He sat next to Zerie and motioned for Vashti to join them. "You need rest still," he told Vashti. "It's tiring getting through this forest."

"I feel great," Vashti said. "Later I'm going to try levitating us for a while. It might be a little bumpy because the trees grow every which way, but that only means it's challenging."

Zerie frowned. She stared at a red heart flower growing near her finger, and she willed it to bloom.

It didn't. Her talent was still gone, and Vashti's was getting stronger every minute.

She shut her eyes and focused on thinking positive

thoughts. She was trying to be good. She was trying to stay out of Vashti's way with Brink.

Maybe it would take a few days for her magic to get stronger again. The only way to get there was to be patient, because patience was a good thing, and magic was good.

Magic was good.

When she opened her eyes, she was alone. Alarmed, Zerie jumped to her feet, almost banging her head on the trunk of the pine tree above her. She must've fallen asleep—she'd kept watch by herself nearly all night, and her body wasn't used to being awake during the day again.

Where were Vashti and Brink? She glanced around. Their packs were still here, close together under the branches of the oak growing about ten feet up the wall. But there was no sign of her friends.

Did they get taken? she thought frantically. *Maybe Ozma's soldiers came while I was asleep and captured them! Why else would they leave their bags behind?*

It didn't make sense, though. If the soldiers had taken her friends, why wouldn't they take her, too?

The answer dawned on her immediately. They hadn't taken her because she didn't have any magic.

Ozma was so powerful, she must know who had talent and who didn't. And Zerie's talent was gone.

I could get it back if I tapped into my bad side, a little voice whispered in her head. *I can use my anger to give me strength, and I can go after the soldiers and age them all until they turn to dust. I can rescue Brink and Vashti!*

Zerie shook her head, hard. She didn't even want such thoughts in her mind. Killing soldiers? Was that what she had become? No good person would even consider something like that, no matter how desperate she was, no matter how many friends had been captured. Maybe Ozma was right to take all the witches and put them in the Forbidden Fountain. Maybe it was the only way to keep Oz safe from people like Zerie.

A peal of laughter caught her attention.

Vashti!

Filled with relief, Zerie rushed toward the sound. Over a tree and under three more, then to the left to work around some thick reddish pine branches . . . and there in front of her lay a shimmering silver stream. Trees grew sideways into the water, forming natural jetties and docks and diving boards. More trees grew at an angle higher up, their pink-tinged leaves making a sort of arched roof overhead. The sun filtered through, sparkling off the water. Iridescent unicorn-flies flitted about, swooping and dipping their rainbow wings in the spray. It was the most beautiful place Zerie had ever seen.

Screaming with laughter, Vashti ran along a pine trunk and launched herself off into the stream one step ahead of Brink, who was chasing her. Zerie caught her breath when she saw him—he'd taken off his shirt and the sight of his bare chest made her heart beat a little faster.

Brink landed with a gigantic splash and grabbed Vashti around the waist, throwing her back into the water as she playfully kicked and squealed.

Zerie felt a stab of jealousy. How could he do that, holding her in his arms one day and now flirting with her best friend two days later?

"Do you have any idea how loud you're being?" she yelled. "I could hear you way back where you left me. In fact, you woke me up!" She knew it was a lie, but she didn't care. "And nice job being on watch, by the way—anybody could have captured me and you two wouldn't even know about it!"

She turned and stalked back the way she'd come before either of them could even respond. Both of them had been staring at her open-mouthed, and she didn't want to hear what they would say when they recovered from their surprise.

Zerie's cheeks were burning.

What did I just do? she thought, slowing down as soon as she knew she was out of sight. *How could I yell at my friends just for having fun? What is wrong with me?*

Back where they'd left their packs, Zerie dropped to the ground and covered her eyes. Maybe she could pretend to be sleeping, and then when they got back, they would think she had been sleepwalking. Or maybe she could pretend she'd been joking around? Anything but admit the truth—she was jealous and mad at them, even though she'd promised herself that she was going to stay out of it! She'd sworn to herself that she would let Vashti have her crush on Brink and she wouldn't interfere.

But I didn't realize I'd have to watch them together, she thought sadly. *I didn't realize Brink liked her as much as she likes him.*

"I'm terrible at being good," she whispered, picturing what Grammy would say. "Not interfering would be the good thing to do, not the easy thing to do. Being good isn't easy."

She was so ashamed of herself that she didn't even look at her friends when they came back a few minutes later. Neither of them said a thing, and she could tell they were mad at her. They just gathered their packs and started walking. Zerie grabbed her stuff and went with them. What else could she do?

It was hard not to feel self-conscious when she still smelled like swamp mud and her clothes were filthy. The two of them had washed themselves clean in the stream. *If I'd joined them instead of yelling at them, I would be clean, too,* she thought. *So I guess I deserve to be dirty.*

"I think I'll try levitation now," Vashti said after an hour or so. "The sun is going down, and we'll run out of light soon. We can get farther faster if we float."

"If you feel strong enough," Brink said in a worried tone.

"I do." Vashti held out both of her hands. Brink took one right away, but Zerie moved more slowly. It felt too intimate to touch her friends after she'd yelled at them both. But Vashti smiled and squeezed Zerie's hand. "Maybe you can make us move even faster while I levitate us," she suggested.

"No, I can't, and you know it!" Zerie snapped,

yanking her hand out of Vashti's. "But thanks for rubbing it in."

"What are you talking about?" Vashti cried.

"I helped us plenty when your talent wasn't doing anything at all," Zerie yelled. "Excuse me if I'm the one who's useless for a little while."

"Zerie!" Brink cried.

"You thought I was useless?" Vashti asked, tears in her eyes. "You said you believed in me. That's why I was finally able to levitate us all, because you kept telling me I could."

"I know." Zerie ran her hand through her hair, trembling. "I did believe in you. I don't know what I'm saying. I'm sorry." She took a shaky breath. "But I can't use my magic to help us because I don't have any left. I should just go home. You two can go to Glinda, and I'll go back to the village. Ozma won't come after me—my talent is gone."

"That's crazy." Vashti's voice sounded like a whip, and Zerie stared at her in shock. "You're just tired because you used too much energy at once, and now you feel sorry for yourself because you're not the strongest one anymore."

"I do not!" Zerie protested. "I just understand it

better now. I let my anger come out and that's how I aged that Kalidah's body. It was negative emotion and so it was negative magic. And now my talent is gone, so I can't use it the way I used to when I was good. And I don't want to use it by being bad."

"You're not being bad. You're just mad at me for some reason," Vashti said. "I think you're jealous."

"I am jealous," Zerie shot back. "I'm jealous of you even though I promised myself I wouldn't be. It won't go away, and it's a bad way to feel, so I should just leave. Like I said I would!"

She spun away, ready to climb up the tree ladder all the way to the top of the forest if she had to. She needed to get out of there right now.

"You're a quitter!" Vashti yelled at her. "I felt the same way you did for the first part of our trip—I couldn't do anything, and you were busy exploding giant feet and saving everybody! Don't you think I was jealous of you, too? But I didn't leave."

"You kept talking about it, though," Zerie snapped.

"But I didn't do it," Vashti spat. "I stuck it out even though you two were so thrilled with yourselves, and now you just have to stick it out, too, whether you like it or not!"

"Stop telling me what to do!" Zerie yelled.

"Stop acting like a baby!" Vashti yelled back.

"Both of you stop," Brink said, his voice cutting through their argument like a knife. Zerie had almost forgotten he was there, and by the look on Vashti's face, it seemed she had as well.

"Stop fighting. Stop acting weird with each other. Just stop!" Brink's tone was furious. "You've been friends forever, and now all you do is fight all the time. You want to stop being jealous of each other? Stop liking the same boy!"

He hurled his pack over his shoulder and stormed off through the Tilted Forest faster than Zerie had ever seen him move before, jumping over huge branches like they were tiny little weeds.

Zerie blinked in astonishment. "I can't believe he said that," she murmured.

"Me either." Vashti wore a stunned expression. "How embarrassing."

"I know." Zerie turned to her friend. "I mean, it's true. Mostly I've been jealous because of . . . you know."

Vashti nodded. "Me too."

"But I really was talking about our talents," Zerie

went on. "I don't want to let all the bad feelings turn me into a bad witch. I'd rather stay like this, with no magic."

"Well . . . maybe Brink's right. Maybe all the bad feelings come from liking the same boy," Vashti said. "Could we just stop liking him, do you think?"

"I can try." Zerie bit her lip. "I really like him a lot."

Vashti frowned.

"Vashti! Zerie! Thank goodness!" A loud voice echoed through the woods. "I've been searching for you for days!"

He came crashing through the branches, his handsome face alight with relief: Ned Springer.

.16.

Ned stopped in front of the two girls, smiling. His brown eyes gleamed, his thick, dark hair was as perfect as ever, and his beautifully muscled arms were held out to them both.

Zerie automatically ran her hand through her curls before remembering that she was still half covered in swamp mud. Somehow the mortifying realization snapped her out of the haze she and Vashti had fallen into.

"It's an illusion, just like last time!" she said, turning to her friend. "Ned's not really here." She raised her voice. "Brink!" she called. "Stop it! You made your point!"

"Brink's here, too?" Ned asked, dropping his arms. His eyebrows knit together in confusion. "What do you mean, it's an illusion?"

Zerie stared at him, confused. Did illusions talk? Had Brink's illusions ever made a sound before? Or was this some new way his talent had grown, like the way Vashti could move when she levitated, or the way she herself could make things age?

"He's real," Vashti whispered, clutching Zerie's hand. "He's really here."

"Of course I am." Ned took another step toward them. "Where's my brother?"

"I'm not sure. He ran off," Zerie said, trying to shake off the weirdness of the situation. It'd been days since she'd even spoken to anyone besides Vashti and Brink, and they were so far away from home, in the middle of the wilderness . . . it was bizarre to be talking to Ned Springer, her clockwork-building fantasy boy from the village. "Ned, what are you doing here?"

"Trying to find you girls, of course." Ned smiled. "There have been search parties out since you ran off. Didn't you know we'd be looking for you?"

Zerie hesitated. She had known people would be looking for them, but she'd assumed that those people were Ozma's spies. It hadn't occurred to her that a village search party would locate them when the Winged Monkeys couldn't. And she wasn't really sure how that could've happened.

"No," she finally said. "We thought our families might try to find us, but—"

"But we didn't think anyone would come this far," Vashti said. "Did you really travel all this way just to find Brink? I knew you would. I knew you'd do anything to make sure your little brother was safe."

Ned nodded, his eyes locked on Vashti's. "I would never stop searching . . . for any of you."

Vashti blushed and giggled. Zerie stared at her in astonishment. Did Vashti still like Ned, after everything that had happened?

"How did you find us, Ned?" Zerie asked. "Is my brother Zepho with you?"

He turned his charming smile on her. "No, Zepho is with a different search party, but you'll see him when you get home."

"But I'm not going home, not yet," Zerie said. "We have to finish what we started. Then we'll come home."

Ned's smile turned into a devastated frown, as if

she'd crushed his dreams. "Zerie, you can't mean that. Do you know how upset your grandmother is? She's been crying night and day."

Zerie felt a rush of sadness. She hated the idea of Grammy crying at all, and that she was the cause of it made things even worse. "But if we go home, we'll be arrested," she said. "Don't you know why we left?"

"I know there were airships, and they took Tabitha away," Ned replied. "But they never came back after that night. You have nothing to be afraid of."

"Really? The Winged Monkeys didn't come looking for us?" Vashti said.

"Of course not." Ned smiled at Vashti again. "Why would they look for you, Vashti? Just because you were friends with Tabitha? We were all fooled by her, not just you."

Fooled by her? Zerie frowned. The last time she'd seen Ned Springer, he had basically admitted that he had a crush on Tabitha. Was he really willing to believe bad things about Tabitha just because Ozma's soldiers told him to?

"I don't know." Vashti shot Zerie a questioning look. "We probably shouldn't go home . . ."

"Vashti." Ned positioned himself between the two girls, staring into Vashti's eyes. "I came all this way to find you. Please don't tell me it was for nothing." He reached out and took her hand. "The longer you stay away from home, the more you're hurting those of us who love you."

"Who love me?" Vashti gasped, flushing.

Zerie stared at her. The Vashti she'd been fighting with five minutes ago had vanished. The strong, fearless Vashti, who'd spent the last two days levitating three people from place to place almost as gracefully as Glinda herself could, had suddenly turned into a giggling, blushing girl with a crush.

A crush on Ned Springer, not Brink Springer.

I can't believe it, Zerie thought. *All this time, I've been assuming Vashti liked Brink, when really she still wants Ned.*

Zerie felt a rush of relief so strong that she laughed out loud. Both Ned and Vashti turned to her, confused.

"Ned!" Brink suddenly appeared, ducking under the tree trunk behind her. "What are you doing here? How could you? How could my own brother betray me this way?"

The relief Zerie had felt was gone. Vashti might not

have a crush on Brink, but Brink obviously still had a crush on her.

A crashing sound in the woods behind Ned made everyone jump. Zerie glanced at the trunk of an oak about twenty feet above them.

A Winged Monkey stood on it, spreading his wings to make another flight. Her heart hammering, she threw her head back and squinted up at the tiny patch of sky visible through the trees. A dark shape blotted out the blue sky.

An airship!

"No!" Zerie cried. "Vashti, the Monkeys!"

She saw Ned Springer's hand tighten on Vashti's. "I was hoping you would just trust me, like Tabitha did," he said. "It would've been easier to take you that way." His smile gone, he pulled her toward him. Vashti's eyes went wide and she struggled . . . until Brink hurled himself at his brother, knocking Ned to the side long enough for Vashti to yank her hand free.

Two more Monkeys dropped from the sky, hopping from tree to tree. It was as hard for them to fly in this forest as it was for Zerie and her friends to walk.

Ned stood up and faced off with Brink. Zerie cringed. Ned was older, and about four inches taller, and he had the heavily muscled shoulders and arms that Zerie had always admired. As cute as Brink was, he still wasn't as big as his older brother.

"Zerie! What do we do?" Vashti cried.

Zerie didn't even think. She simply moved—fast—grabbing Vashti by the arm and then running for Brink. She pulled him away from his brother before Ned could even react, and then she ran, leaping over the tree trunks, dragging her friends along with her.

"Levitate us," she said as she ran. "Up into the thickest treetop you can see."

"You have to slow down," Vashti cried. "I can't see the trees!"

Zerie was moving so fast that she had no idea how far they'd gone from Ned and the Winged Monkeys. Still, she didn't want to stop until she was sure they were safe.

"Zerie, slow down!" Brink sounded desperate.

She forced herself to stop, suddenly realizing that the two of them were getting banged around as she dragged them. "Sorry," she said.

And then her feet left the ground and she floated up, up, up with Vashti and Brink, weaving through the reddish tree trunks and around the interlocking branches until finally they came to rest in the crotch of a tall pine tree that grew almost straight up toward the sun. Below it was an ancient, hoary oak that grew sideways, its branches spreading out below their perch like a safety net.

"The Monkeys can fly," Vashti whispered. "We might be above Ned, but the Monkeys will be able to find us."

Zerie looked down at the dizzying view beneath them—an entire sideways forest. Between the trees, at least thirty Winged Monkeys flitted about, leaping from branch to branch, shrieking to one another. Searching for Zerie and her friends.

"They'll be here in another minute," Zerie said.

"I don't know what else to do," Vashti replied.

"I do," Brink said. He gazed at the pink pine leaves in front of them, his face going blank. Vashti shot Zerie a frightened look, but Zerie knew it would be okay. Brink was making an illusion.

A Monkey shot up from the tree beneath them, appearing so suddenly that Vashti almost fell off the branch. Zerie caught her and slapped her hand over her friend's mouth to stifle her scream. "Watch," she breathed into Vashti's ear.

They both stared at the Winged Monkey, who had come to rest on the end of the same branch they sat on. The Monkey stared back at them from three feet away.

Vashti dug her fingers into Zerie's arm so hard that it hurt, and Zerie held her breath. Brink kept staring at the leaves, not even glancing at the Monkey, who was close enough to touch him. Nobody moved.

Zerie looked into the creature's large black eyes, searching for a reflection. He was looking back at her—she should have seen her own face. Instead all she saw was leaves, branches . . . trees, but no people.

The Winged Monkey shrieked, communicating something to its companions, and then spread its wings, each leathery fold stretching closer and closer to Brink's face. Zerie bit her lip, forcing herself to stay quiet.

The monkey leapt from the tree, taking off into midair and circling down to another one, and then another lower still.

"What was that?" Vashti whispered.

"He didn't see us, he saw an illusion," Zerie said. "He saw branches and leaves, a thick treetop."

"But he was looking straight at us," Vashti protested.

"But he didn't see us," Brink replied.

"How long can you hold the illusion?" Zerie asked. Brink's shoulders were tense, and she could tell that it took an effort to make such a good illusion. She reached over and put her hand on his arm. He relaxed a little and looked back at her.

"For a while, as long as we don't move," he said. "The hardest part is making it in the first place."

Vashti let out a long, shuddering breath. "So we're safe."

"For now." Brink's expression was grim. "We just have to stay here and hope they give up."

"I can't believe Ned is working with the Winged Monkeys," Vashti said. "Why would he do that? He must think they're right and that going back home is what's best for us."

"No!" Brink exploded. "It's just like I always suspected! He's working with them because he always has been. Can't you see that? I never wanted to believe it before, but Ned is a spy. He's the one who told them where to find us in the first place, back in the woods at home."

Brink ran his fingers angrily though his sandy hair, and Zerie could see that his hands were shaking. "He loved building clockwork birds and flies, but I never saw him selling them to anyone," he said, his voice tense. "When the Glass Cat talked about clockwork spies, I wondered if Ned could be making them. But I didn't think it could be true. We were never close, but I didn't think he'd turn in his own brother."

"He told me he liked Tabitha," Zerie said, stunned. "But he was lying; he wanted to find out where Tabitha would be so he could capture her. He must've seen her doing magic at her house."

"What?" Vashti cried. "When did he say he liked Tabitha? I can't believe you didn't tell me that."

"Really? That's what you care about?" Brink asked incredulously. "Who he likes? He's the one who put us in this mess! Everything that's happened is his fault, and you two are still willing to fight over him? Stop it. Stop liking my brother. He doesn't deserve it."

Vashti turned red. "You're right."

Brink turned to Zerie, eyebrows raised.

"I don't like your brother," she said. "I haven't since that day you made an illusion of him."

"Oh." Brink looked confused. "Well . . . good."

They all sat silently for a while, watching as the Monkeys circled, screeching in their strange language.

"Zerie, you used your talent," Vashti finally said. "I knew you still had it. You saved us. Again."

"We all saved us," Zerie said. "All three of us did it together."

"We're strongest that way. Friends are always strongest together," Brink put in, and Zerie nodded.

"So you were wrong about the bad energy stuff," Vashti said. "Because you must've been angry when you pulled us away from Ned."

"I was angry." Zerie frowned. "But that's what I wanted to avoid—using my anger to fuel my talent. I think using bad emotions like anger means that the magic I'm doing is bad. I think that's what led the Wicked Witches to be wicked."

"But you had no choice. If you hadn't sped us out of there, the Monkeys would have captured us," Brink said. "So the magic you did was good, even if it was anger that gave you the power to do it."

"I have a different idea," Vashti said. "I don't think it's as simple as good feelings make good magic and bad feelings make bad magic. I think if you feel bad about yourself, you're just not as powerful."

"How do you mean?" Zerie asked.

"Well, I couldn't figure out how my talent was

useful for the longest time. You both used your talents to escape the night they took Tabitha, but I didn't. Mine felt worthless," Vashti said. "And then you and I were so awkward because of all that stuff with Ned, Zerie. I just felt bad about myself, and about us . . . and every time I tried to use my talent, it didn't work so well."

"The same way mine wasn't working after we killed the Kalidah," Zerie said. "I felt awful after that, because I killed something. And then . . ." Her voice trailed off. She'd been about to say that then she thought Brink and Vashti liked each other and it made her jealous, but that seemed too embarrassing to talk about.

"I guess I'm the only one who always likes myself," Brink said, his old teasing smile on his face. "My talent has been working the whole time!"

Zerie laughed, and so did Vashti.

"Maybe you're right. Maybe it's more that our emotions affect our magical abilities," Zerie said. "Grammy always told me that magic came from feeling good. Maybe she just meant that being happy was the way to have strong magic. And then being sad, or angry, or jealous—that's the path to weak magic."

"Were you happy when you rescued us from Ned?" Brink asked.

Zerie thought about it. "No. I was angry, but it was because he'd betrayed us. I was right to be angry about that."

"You were right to be angry about the Kalidah, too," Vashti said gently. "You were mad that Ozma's rules put us in a position where we had to kill a living thing. I'm angry at Ozma for that just like you are."

"So am I," Brink agreed.

"Then it was my guilt that made my power go away," Zerie said, filled with relief. "Oh, you don't know how happy that makes me. I was afraid I would turn into a Wicked Witch!"

They all laughed.

"You know what? I haven't heard any Winged Monkeys for a while," Vashti said. "Do you think they're gone?"

Zerie looked up at the sky while Vashti peered down into the forest. "I don't see the airship anymore, though it's hard to tell through the trees," Zerie said.

"I don't see any Monkeys," Vashti reported.

"We'd better wait, though," Brink said. "They could be hiding, hoping we'll come out and reveal ourselves. I can keep the illusion going. It's easier now that we're all friends again. I feel stronger."

"You know why?" Zerie asked

"Because friends are always strongest together," Vashti and Brink answered at the same time. All three of them laughed.

"It's getting dark. If we're going to be here all night, I'm going to sleep," Vashti announced. "Zerie had a nap before, and Brink will have to sleep after we know we're safe and he can stop the illusion."

"Good idea," Zerie said. "Can you sleep in a tree?"

Vashti yawned. "Just catch me if I start to fall."

For about a half hour, everything was quiet. Zerie searched the sky and the trees below, but nothing moved in the gathering dusk. "How long until we know they're gone?" she finally said.

"I have no idea," Brink admitted.

"I'm sorry about Ned," Zerie told him. "I can't imagine how I'd feel if one of my brothers or sisters did something like that."

Brink shrugged. "You're close to your siblings. Ned and I have never been close. I could never figure out what you two saw in him."

Zerie thought about it. "He was cute," she said.

Brink stared at her. "That's it?"

"Pretty much." Zerie felt her cheeks heat up. "I know how stupid it sounds. A lot of the things I used to think seem stupid now."

"You said you haven't liked Ned since we left our village," Brink said awkwardly. "So what were you and Vashti fighting about?"

Zerie couldn't look him in the eye. "Well, we were fighting about our talents and how we were jealous of each other. And I guess she thought we were still fighting about Ned, too, and how we both liked him. And I thought . . ." She took a deep breath. "I thought we were fighting about you and how we both liked you."

"Oh." Brink squirmed around a bit, as if he was uncomfortable. "But Vashti still liked Ned."

"Yeah, that was a surprise," Zerie admitted. "It's so complicated, isn't it? We both liked Ned, but he liked Tabitha. Well, I guess that was a lie. But then I liked you but you liked Vashti, and Vashti still liked Ned. We should all just stop being so silly."

"I never liked Vashti," Brink said. "Not that way."

"What do you mean?" Zerie asked, turning to face him.

"I mean I like *you*, Zerie," Brink said. "I always have."

Zerie gazed at him, speechless.

"Am I interrupting anything?" the Glass Cat asked, jumping down from the tree above them. She landed lightly on the branch Vashti slept on and blinked at them with her emerald eyes. "I certainly hope not, because it's time for us to go."

.17.

"Where did you come from?" Zerie cried. "Never mind, I always ask you that and you never answer."

"But how did you find us?" Brink asked. "I'm still holding the illusion of branches and leaves. How could you see through it? Is the illusion fading?"

"May I remind you, I am a cat," said the cat. "And I am also a magical creature. I know better than to trust my eyes. I could smell Zerie a mile away. Swamp mud."

Zerie's hand flew to her mouth in horror. She'd completely forgotten about the swamp mud.

"And you others aren't very sweet-smelling, either,"

the cat went on. "Humans are all stinky. You should be more like cats. We're very clean creatures."

Zerie frowned. "Why didn't the Winged Monkeys smell us, then? There was one sitting right here a while back."

The cat laughed her delicate laugh. "It probably did smell you. But it couldn't see you and so it didn't understand. The Monkeys aren't as intelligent as I am, after all. They believe their eyes. I believe my intuition."

"You're back," Vashti said groggily, sitting up. "I thought I was dreaming."

"That's very understandable," the Glass Cat said. "I would make a brilliant dream."

"Where have you been?" Brink asked. "Why did you disappear for so long? We had a lot of trouble in The Trenches."

The cat sat up very straight and glared at him. "I go where I please," she spat, offended.

"Okay, okay, don't get all mad about it. We've all decided to stop being angry at one another," Zerie said. "What did you mean when you said it's time for us to go now?"

"The Winged Monkeys are gone—the airship left,"

the cat replied. "But they know that you are some-where within the Tilted Forest, so most likely, they will be back soon with many more airships. You can't stay here."

"I didn't even think of that," Brink said.

"Glinda's Palace is only a short march away. If we leave now, we can be there by morning." The cat stood and stretched herself. "Let's go."

Zerie looked at her friends. "I guess we're going."

"You might have to levitate me there while I sleep, Vashti," Brink grumbled. "I've been working an illusion for hours now. I'm exhausted."

Zerie wanted to take his hand to comfort him. She wanted to continue their conversation from before the cat had arrived. She wanted to hug him, or kiss him, or something. He'd told her that he liked her!

But the Winged Monkeys were coming back, and they had one last dash to make before they were safe. Talking to Brink would have to wait. They had to focus on getting to Glinda now.

"The road of yellow brick runs next to this forest," the Glass Cat told them. "The forest is like a gash in the land, and the road was built alongside it since it would've been too hard to put the road inside the woods. The road is the only route to Glinda's Palace, because there is a raging river that surrounds her home like a moat. The road becomes a golden bridge that spans the river."

"We're near the top now. We can see a lot of the sky," Vashti said. "Are you saying that if we just get out of the trench that the forest is in, the road will be right there?"

The cat gave her an arch look. "I thought I did just say that."

Vashti made a face at her. "What I mean is, can I levitate us right up to the road?"

"I don't know. Can you?" the cat asked.

"I've learned a lot since you left," Vashti said, taking hold of Zerie and Brink. Zerie smiled and reached for Brink's other hand, but he shot her an apologetic look. He picked up the Glass Cat instead. Zerie was surprised that the cat let him.

Vashti kept her face to the sky as she lifted them gently into the air. She maneuvered them around the trunks of oaks and the reddish branches of pine trees, slowly floating upward.

Zerie felt as if she were in a hot air balloon, like the Wizard of Oz when he first came to Oz. Beneath her feet, the Tilted Forest lay spread out like a painting in the moonlight, and soon enough, the only thing above them was the sky.

The road of yellow brick glowed softly in the night.

Vashti placed them down on the bricks, and Zerie felt the same thrill that she'd always felt at the idea of this road—although now it was mixed with trepidation. The last time they'd been on the road, Ozma's mounted cavalry had been patrolling. "I wish you could fly us all the way to Glinda's Palace," she told Vashti.

"I'm not strong enough for that yet, not if it's still several miles away," Vashti replied. "Though maybe if you moved us really fast, I could do it. We said we're all strongest when we use our magic together."

"You will find that your talents won't work as well the closer you get to Glinda," the cat said. "She is such a powerful sorceress that the entire landscape around her palace is enchanted. That is how she protects herself from the magic of others. Her enchantment is stronger than your talent, or anyone's talent. Even the Wicked Witches would have had a hard time using their magic within Glinda's Palace."

"Then we'll have to walk, and walk quickly," Zerie

said. She linked one arm through Vashti's, and her other arm through Brink's. "I'll use my talent to make us go faster . . . for as long as it works."

They set off moving at a good pace, much faster than anyone could walk on their own. But after about an hour, Zerie began to feel heavy. Her eyelids felt heavy, her feet felt heavy, and the friends hanging on to her arms felt heavy. "I can't go on," she said, exhausted. "I think this is how Dorothy the explorer must've felt in the poppy fields."

"It's the enchantment. Glinda's land must be close by," the Glass Cat said. "If you stop trying to fight it by using your talent, you may feel better."

Zerie let her eyelids close, and her leaden feet stop moving. Instead of moving fast, she allowed herself to stop altogether. With a sigh, she gave up on her talent. She wouldn't need it once they were under Glinda's protection, anyway.

"Zerie?" Brink sounded concerned.

"I'm okay." She opened her eyes and smiled at him. "I had to sort of turn my magic off. I do feel more awake now, just like the cat said."

"From here on, we're all regular citizens of Oz with no magical talents," Vashti said. "But we should still hurry. I think Ozma's Winged Monkeys are allowed to chase us right up to Glinda's door if they want."

"It's true," Zerie said as they linked arms and began walking again, "we don't know for sure that Glinda will even be willing to help us. What if we've come all this way for nothing?"

"It wasn't for nothing," Brink said, squeezing her arm. "We got closer to each other."

Zerie felt a flutter in her stomach, and she squeezed his arm back.

"Plus, we learned so much about our talents," Vashti put in. "I feel sure now that I won't let Ozma take away my magic, even if Glinda doesn't help us. I'll fight to keep my talent, no matter what."

"Me too," said Zerie. "But I really hope Glinda will help."

"There's the palace," the Glass Cat announced. "In the midst of the pink haze you see in the distance. Every morning, just before dawn, that pink haze gathers around Glinda's Palace. When the sun comes up, the pink clouds float up into the sky and the entire castle is revealed."

"That sounds beautiful," Vashti breathed.

"If you like that sort of thing," the cat replied.

As they walked closer, the strange haze enveloped them, and Zerie found that she could see everything in front of her clearly. But when she turned to look back the way they'd come, the road of yellow brick was hidden in the pink haze. It was as if they'd stepped into a bubble of pink that surrounded Glinda's Palace—from the outside, you couldn't see in, and from the inside, you couldn't see out.

"Where's the cat?" Brink asked, looking around.

Startled, Zerie scanned the area. "She's gone again. Did she come into the pink haze?"

"I don't see her," Vashti replied.

Zerie shook her head. She would never understand what went on in the strange pink brain of that cat.

"This place is even more gorgeous than I'd heard," Vashti said. "How many turrets does the palace have?"

"I count at least seven," Brink replied. "And look at the dome in the middle!"

Zerie didn't contribute to the conversation. She simply stared at the stunning castle, taking in the white marble towers, the pink marble windowsills and rooftops, and the delicate veins of gold running through the entire building.

She could hardly believe they'd finally made it.

"There's the bridge." Brink pointed ahead to where the road of yellow brick took a sharp turn and narrowed into a golden pathway. The path left land and leapt in a delicate arch over white, rushing water.

"Let's run," Brink suggested. "The palace gates are just on the other side of the bridge."

Zerie stopped in her tracks, and so did Vashti. "Brink," she said. "We can't cross that bridge."

"What do you mean? Why not?" he asked.

"Because it's missing a middle!" Vashti cried. "The whole center of the archway is gone!"

"Oh, no," Zerie moaned. "The monkeys must've gotten here before us and knocked down Glinda's bridge so we couldn't reach her."

"What are you talking about?" Brink said. "The bridge is fine."

"Are you telling me that you can see a bridge there?" Zerie asked him. "A whole bridge?"

"Of course. It's an arch. It goes all the way across the raging river," Brink said. "Are you telling me that you can't see that?"

"I see a broken bridge," Vashti said.

"Me too." Zerie frowned. "Is it part of the enchantment?"

"If it is, it's not working on me," Brink said.

"Well, maybe it is and you're seeing things that aren't there," Vashti told him.

They all studied the bridge in silence for a moment.

"It's an illusion," Brink finally said. "You see a broken bridge, and so you don't try to cross it. It's just one more protection to keep evildoers from entering Glinda's Palace."

"Are you calling us evildoers?" Zerie demanded.

"No, of course not. I just mean that Glinda must keep the illusion there all the time." Brink shrugged. "I think I can just see through the illusion because that's my talent, making illusions."

"None of our talents work within Glinda's enchantment, that's what the cat said." Zerie looked at Brink doubtfully.

"Well . . ." Brink's gaze unfocused for a moment, the way it did when he used his magic. "I can't make an illusion, so my talent isn't working. But I definitely see the bridge."

"That doesn't make sense," Vashti said.

"Maybe not, but I'm certain of it." Brink took a step out onto the archway, and Zerie gasped. "I'm so certain," he added, "that I'm going to prove it to you."

"Brink, no!" Zerie cried as he moved closer to the gap in the bridge. "You'll be swept away in the river!"

Brink turned back and met her eye, smiling as he gazed at her. "Zerie," he said. "You know how I feel about you. I would never put you in danger."

With that, he turned and ran toward Glinda's Palace. Zerie stifled a scream as his foot stepped off the edge of the golden bridge . . . and then he was running in midair, up the line of the arch and down the other side, until his feet were on the golden path again.

"I still don't see the bridge," Vashti said.

"Neither do I, but Brink is across the river," Zerie replied. "Unless he suddenly learned to levitate like you, the bridge must really be there."

"I'm scared," Vashti whispered, grabbing on to Zerie's hand.

"Me too," Zerie said. Together they walked out onto the bridge, inching closer and closer to the gap. When they got to the edge, Zerie peered down. Fifty feet below, the river raged, eddies and whitecaps marring its surface. To fall in there would be certain death, and she could see nothing in between her and the river.

"I can't do this," Vashti whimpered. "Not without my talent. If I could only levitate us across, I don't think that I would be scared, but this is terrifying."

Zerie swallowed down the lump in her throat. "It's just an illusion. Think of how real Ned looked when Brink made that illusion. Think of the way the Winged Monkey stared right at us and didn't see us. Illusions are powerful."

"If you say so." Vashti's whole body was shaking. "But I can't look." She closed her eyes.

Zerie didn't want to look down at the river, either. Instead she gazed ahead to where Brink stood at the base of the bridge on the other side. Behind him were the golden doors of Glinda's Palace. Brink smiled encouragingly at her, his expression loving. "It's okay, Zerie," he called. "Trust me."

That's what Ned said to Tabitha before he betrayed her, Zerie thought.

But Brink wasn't the same as his brother. Brink was honest, and good, and he cared about Zerie. He'd told her so.

"I do trust you," she said. Summoning all her courage, she stepped off the edge of the bridge, hoping to feel solid gold beneath her when her foot came down.

Instead there was a screech, and darkness filled the sky. Black leathery hands grabbed her arms in a grip like iron, and she was lifted into the air.

Vashti screamed, and her hand was jerked out of Zerie's grip. Terrified, Zerie watched as her best friend was carried away by a Winged Monkey. Twisting around, she saw that a Monkey had her by both arms, too. Its wings made a mighty wind as they flapped, carrying her upward to the airship that floated above them.

"No!" Zerie yelled. Frantically, she searched for Brink, and spotted him still standing where he'd been before, in front of Glinda's gates, shielding his eyes as he watched the Winged Monkeys take her away.

He had lured her out onto the bridge, where there was no protection. He'd made her feel safe, just like Ned had made Tabitha feel safe.

Brink had betrayed her.

.18.

"Do you think Tabitha is still here somewhere?" Vashti asked as they gazed out the emerald-tinted windows of the giant airship an hour later. The Monkeys hadn't wasted any time once they dragged the girls into the airship. They'd simply chained their legs and arms together and shoved them both into a small room with a locked door. The huge ship had begun moving immediately afterward. "It's been a long time. Maybe they've already taken away her magic and sent her back home."

"I don't know," Zerie murmured. She stared out at the Land of Oz drifting by far below them—the road of yellow brick twining through the reddish wilderness of Quadling Country like a golden snake, The Trenches with their strange lines of landscape, Big Enough Mountain in the distance. From up here, nothing looked as dangerous as it had been on the ground.

Zerie wished all these places didn't hold so many memories, because most of those memories involved Brink.

"Why didn't the Winged Monkeys take Brink, too?" Vashti asked. "If he's one of them . . ."

Zerie shrugged. "Ned isn't on the ship, either. Maybe only monkeys are allowed on the ships," she said. The truth was, she didn't really care about any of these questions. The weight of the chains they'd put on her arms and legs felt like nothing compared to the weight on her heart. She'd finally let herself be honest with Brink about her feelings, and he said he felt the same way . . . but it was a lie.

"It's not fair. They're treating us like criminals, chaining us up." Vashti sounded angry, but Zerie just felt resigned. She didn't even care if they put her into the Water of Oblivion and erased all her memories.

She didn't want to remember anything about Brink.

"They have to chain us up to make sure that we don't try to use our talents to escape," she told Vashti.

Vashti sighed. "I'm sorry about Brink," she said. "I know you two had . . . something."

"I thought we did. He said we did." Zerie shook her head. "Why can't it be simpler? Why can't people just be one thing all the time and not change?"

"I don't know. But you've changed, and I've changed," Vashti said. "Maybe nobody is only one thing, only good or only bad. We've managed to be a little bit of both since we left home."

Zerie smiled and reached for Vashti's hand. "We won't forget each other, right? Even in the Forbidden Fountain, we'll remember that we're best friends and we always were."

"And we always will be," Vashti promised.

The airship shuddered and began sinking, and the girls heard more screeching from the Winged Monkeys outside the little room where they were being held.

"We're almost there," Zerie said, looking out the window. "I see the Emerald City."

Vashti gazed out at the tall green walls, the many green spires and towers. "It's not as big as I thought it would be," she said. "Though I guess it will look plenty big once we're in the middle of it."

She was right. The city was huge.

When the airship landed, the Monkeys escorted them down the gangplank into the middle of the city square. The enormous gold-and-emerald gates of the Royal Palace took up one entire side of the square.

Zerie had imagined that there would be a crowd of people there to watch them, or yell at them, or both. But the entire square was empty except for one man.

"It's the Wizard," Vashti said, clutching Zerie's arm.

They walked toward the old man, their footsteps echoing off the tall green buildings that surrounded them. From down here, the houses and public halls did seem big, and somehow the emptiness made them feel ominous.

"Where is everyone?" Zerie whispered.

"You do not need to face the citizens of the Emerald City, Zerie Greenapple," the Wizard answered, his voice close by even though he still stood halfway across the square.

"How did he hear you?" Vashti cried.

"I am the Wizard of Oz, my dear. I am very

powerful," his voice said again. "My ways are mysterious and not for you to question."

Zerie felt a bolt of anger shoot through her. She wrenched her arm out of the grasp of the monkey who held her and stalked forward as fast as she could with the chains around her ankles.

She stormed right up to the Wizard and stuck her face close to his.

"If you're so powerful that we can't question you, then why do you get to question us for being powerful?" she demanded. "Why should you have the right to use magic but we don't?"

"Zerie!" Vashti cried. "What are you doing? That's the Wizard!"

"I don't care." Zerie knew she was supposed to show respect for the man who was one of Ozma's closest friends, a respected magician trained by Glinda herself. But right now all she could think about was how unfair it was that she and Vashti stood here in chains. "We haven't done anything wrong," she insisted.

The Wizard raised one gray eyebrow and turned his gaze to Vashti.

"Well . . . we killed a Kalidah," Vashti admitted,

voice trembling. "We had no choice. But it was wrong, and we knew it was wrong, and we felt terrible."

The Wizard nodded, and all of Zerie's anger evaporated. Vashti was right. They had done that one terrible thing, and it was terrible enough that maybe they deserved to be punished.

"Zerie and Vashti, you stand accused of using magic in defiance of the laws of Princess Ozma, the rightful ruler of the Land of Oz," the Wizard boomed, his voice bouncing from the walls of the empty square. "According to those laws, therefore, you are hereby sentenced to bathe in the Water of Oblivion within the Forbidden Fountain."

Vashti let out a sob, and Zerie realized that her own cheeks were wet with tears.

The Wizard glanced at the Winged Monkeys. "You can remove their chains now," he said, lowering his voice. "They won't try to use their talents here."

The Monkeys unlocked the chains, and Vashti threw herself into Zerie's arms. "We'll stick together," she said.

"Always," Zerie agreed.

Now that the Wizard had sentenced them, the vast gates of the Royal Palace began to open, swinging slowly and silently outward until they took up half the area of the square. Next a long line of green-coated soldiers marched forth in tight formation, taking their places on either side of Zerie and Vashti, and in a line behind them.

"Let the sentence be carried out!" the Wizard boomed.

The soldiers began to march, and the girls had no choice but to walk toward the palace or be trampled.

The square was empty, but Zerie got the feeling that thousands of eyes were watching her walk from behind the blank walls. This seemed like a lot of pomp for an empty courtyard. One or two soldiers would've been enough.

And why did the Wizard keep speaking so formally and so loudly? Whenever he used his normal voice, he was actually sort of nice to them.

It must be an illusion, she thought. *The square might be full of people, but we can't see them.*

The Wizard caught her eye and gave the slightest wink. "You young girls are frightened enough," he said quietly. "There's no need for you to see the hordes out looking for a witch trial."

"That's a big illusion, hiding all the people," Zerie

said as the palace gates closed behind them. "Brink couldn't do anything like that."

"Maybe he never had any talent at all," Vashti replied. "Maybe it was always just the Wizard working magic that would fool us into trusting Brink."

Zerie frowned. She didn't know what to think anymore. The Wizard was being friendly but sentencing them to certain doom. The Emerald City was filled with people but looked empty. Brink had held her in his arms but betrayed her to the enemy.

"Zerie, look!" Vashti pointed ahead.

They were marching through the main garden of the Royal Palace of Oz, and everything was laid out in a dizzying pattern of diamonds and circles overlapping. The bricks of the pathway were green, and every flower on every plant was green, and the stonework that made up the gigantic fountain in the center of the garden was green marble encrusted with emeralds.

But the water that bubbled up from within was crystal clear.

"The Forbidden Fountain," the Wizard told them, stretching out his arm to allow the girls to step in front of him.

And there, in front of the fountain, stood Tabitha.

Their old friend was as beautiful as ever, with her silky golden hair pulled up into a net strung with emeralds and pearls. She was dressed in a gown of gold and green velvet, as if she had become a part of this place. Tabitha smiled as they approached.

The soldiers marched Zerie and Vashti up to the low wall of the fountain, and then retreated, marching into a circle formation around the Forbidden Fountain, with the girls and Tabitha inside and the Wizard on the outside.

"Tabitha," Zerie cried, reaching to hug her friend. But Tabitha took a step back, and Zerie's arms fell to her sides.

"Tabitha. Don't you remember us?" Vashti asked. "Oh, no. Zerie, what if we forget each other?"

"Please don't worry," Tabitha said with a serene smile. "This is all for the best. You'll see."

"But . . . you're not you anymore," Zerie told her. "Are you?"

Tabitha didn't answer, instead gesturing to the fountain. "Don't fight the movement of the water," she said. "If you give yourself up to the fountain, all will be revealed. It is of vital importance that you obey what you read." She shot Zerie a strange look as she spoke, but then turned away again with that bland smile.

"Prisoners! Approach the Forbidden Fountain," the head soldier commanded. He and all the other soldiers in the circle took two steps inward, crowding the girls closer to the fountain wall.

Zerie leaned over the low wall and looked down. The basin was made of pure gold, gleaming in the sunshine. And on the lip of the fountain wall lay a small plaque.

"All Persons are Forbidden to Drink at this Fountain," Zerie read.

"Enter the fountain!" the head soldier barked. They all took two more steps inward, leaving the girls no room to stand. There was no choice but to climb into the fountain.

Obey what you read, Zerie thought as the water in the golden bowl began to swirl in a circle. It was such an odd thing for Tabitha to say.

"Vashti," she said as her feet hit the icy cold water. "Keep your mouth closed. Don't drink the water, that's what the sign said."

"But they're putting us in the fountain. Isn't that sign for people who haven't been sentenced?" Vashti asked, her teeth chattering from the cold. Her hand clung tightly to Zerie's.

"I don't know. But try not to drink. Maybe it won't work if we don't drink." Zerie's teeth were chattering, too, and she felt as if she couldn't breathe. The Water of Oblivion was cold, so cold, and it was stealing her strength.

"Zerie . . ." Vashti's voice was frightened, and then suddenly Vashti fell, landing in the water with a splash. It hadn't looked so deep from outside the fountain. The current pulled her away, wrenching her hand out of Zerie's, and she was gone.

I don't want to forget my magic, Zerie thought, and then the swirling water knocked her legs out from beneath her, and she was caught in a spiral, being pulled down, down, down in the Water of Oblivion.

The cold water closed over her head.

Everything went black.

.19.

"Zerie Greenapple! It's time to wake up!"

"I don't want to get up, Grammy," Zerie murmured. "I'm so tired . . ."

A light, tinkling sound filled the room, and Zerie frowned in her sleep. That didn't sound like the willow tree scratching at the window. It sounded like a girl laughing. There had been a girl in her bedroom once, waking her up. Tabitha.

"Tabitha!" Zerie bolted awake, sitting straight up in bed.

Except she wasn't in bed. She was sitting, drenched, on the sand in a strange green cave. The roof and walls were made of dark stone with veins of glowing green snaking through it in all directions, and the sand itself was green. The water lapping at her feet, though, was crystal clear and bracingly cold.

Zerie blinked at the water, a vast lake filling nearly the entire length of this huge cavern.

"Here you are, my dear—this will make you warm," said the girl with the tinkling laugh. She placed a warm golden blanket around Zerie's shoulders, and Zerie snuggled into it, gazing up at this young girl with an impossibly beautiful face. Her lips were a rich pink, her eyes sparkled like diamonds, and her blond hair glowed like fire in the dark cave.

Zerie didn't need to look at the tiara on her head to know who this girl was. "Princess Ozma," she said.

"Indeed I am. And you are Zerie Greenapple," said Ozma. "I've been watching you for a long time."

Zerie frowned, trying to remember how she'd gotten here. She looked around. Vashti was on the sand next to her, also wrapped in a blanket, and smiling at her. She saw Tabitha sitting next to Vashti, holding her hand.

And Zerie remembered every single thing she'd ever known about both of them.

The Fountain hadn't erased her memories.

"You outlawed magic, and we were sentenced to the Forbidden Fountain," Zerie said, turning back to Ozma.

"Yes. Only I know the source of the Forbidden Fountain. I discovered this cave many years ago, and I told no one," Ozma replied. "As long as you don't drink the Water of Oblivion, you don't forget yourself. But you can ride the water down to its source."

"I don't understand," Zerie said.

"I'm sorry I had to put you through so much fear, but it was the only way," Ozma replied. "My ban was not to truly forbid the use of magic, but to find out those who had it. Only with the resources of the Winged Monkeys and my other spies could I find those citizens of Oz who possessed a talent for magic. And only by pretending to take away their talent could I protect them."

"Protect us?" Zerie asked. "Protect us from what?"

Ozma's beautiful face grew sad. "The Land of Oz is under attack by a greater evil than it has ever known. This evil is powerful in the ways of magic. So only those with magic can help me fight it."

"You mean, you were looking for us so you could

ask for help?" Vashti asked. "Not so you could remove our magic?"

"Princess Ozma would never steal anyone's inborn talent," Tabitha replied. "But our enemy would. That's why you needed protection. We all must pretend that our magic has been taken, while in secret we must practice until our talents are as strong as they can be."

Zerie could hardly believe her ears. "All this time, everything we thought we knew was inside-out."

Ozma nodded. "Will you help me save Oz?" she asked.

"Of course," Zerie cried.

"We'll do anything," Vashti agreed.

"Thank you, girls. But it is dangerous," Ozma cautioned them. "My enemy cannot know that I am gathering this circle of companions."

"We've faced a lot of danger recently," Zerie told her. "We can handle it. But may I know, Princess, who this terrible enemy is?"

"It is the great sorceress herself," Ozma replied. "Glinda."

"Glinda?" Vashti gasped. "But we were going to her for help! We were going to give ourselves to her. We went right up to her palace, and we didn't even have our talents there. We would have been trapped, helpless!"

"That is precisely why my soldiers took you before you could reach her," Ozma said.

Zerie felt as if the cavern was spinning, and she couldn't catch her breath. "Brink," she said, terrified. "Brink was at the gates of Glinda's Palace. You didn't take him. He would have gone to Glinda and . . . and . . ."

"Once he crossed the bridge, my soldiers could not touch him," Ozma said sadly. "I'm afraid our enemy has captured Brink Springer."

"I thought he betrayed me," Zerie said. "But instead I left him there alone, to face the greatest betrayal of all. He thought he would get help from Glinda."

Princess Ozma placed a small hand on Zerie's shoulder. "My heart aches at his loss," she said.

"No." Zerie stood up, sure of what she had to do. "He's not lost, Princess. I'm going to save him. I will do whatever it takes to rescue Brink."

"Then we'll help you," Tabitha said. She came over and took Zerie's hand.

Vashti took Zerie's other hand. "Of course we will."

"Thank you." Zerie smiled at her two best friends. "I know that between the three of us, we'll find a way."

"Of course you will," Princess Ozma said gently. "Friends are always strongest together."

Laura J. Burns

Laura J. Burns has written more than thirty books for kids and teens, touching on topics from imaginary lake monsters to out-of-control Hollywood starlets. She has also written for the TV shows *Roswell*, *1-800-MISSING,* and *The Dead Zone*. Laura lives in New York with her husband, her kids, and her two exceptionally silly dogs.